ACCLAIM FOR *On the Proper Use of Stars*

Shortlisted for the Governor General's Literary Award for
French to English Translation
A Top 10 Book of the Year, *Montreal Mirror*

IN ITS ORIGINAL EDITION, *Du bon usage des étoiles* (Éditions Alto, 2008)

Shortlisted for the Governor General's Award for Fiction
Finalist, Prix des libraires du Québec
Finalist, Grand prix littéraire Archambault
Finalist, Prix Senghor du premier roman

"Fortier — beautifully translated by Sheila Fischman — takes a new approach [to the Franklin story]: She chooses elegance. . . . Satisfying."
— *Toronto Star*

"[The Arctic] is a subject tackled with compelling elegance by Montreal writer Dominique Fortier. *On the Proper Use of Stars* . . . will please adventurers and romantics."
— Montreal *Mirror*

"It is not every day that one reads great literature. . . . Dominique Fortier has lit a beacon destined to shine for a long time."
— *Voir* magazine (Montreal)

"[Fortier's] stellar talent sparkles: her eclectic culture, her irresistible imagination, her playful sense of humour. . . . Her first novel is a shimmering hall of mirrors."
— *L'actualité*

"[The tale] is told in utterly original fashion, a historical novel with wit and fascination. Fans of Arctic literature will not want to pass on this one."
— *Sun Times* (Owen Sound)

"Fortier has created a seamless tapestry of diary entries and third-person narration, supplemented by a bricolage of scientific diagrams, handwritten letters, poems, recipes, astrological maps of the heavens, musical scores and the like. . . . Fortier's clever, confident prose and Fischman's flawless translation also adopt the literary styles of the era, shifting effortlessly between the comedy of manners of London society and the Gothic romance of the Artic wilderness."
— *National Post*

D1484570

On the
PROPER USE
of STARS

DOMINIQUE FORTIER
translated by SHEILA FISCHMAN

EMBLEM

First English language edition published 2010
Emblem edition published 2011

Originally published as *Du bon usage des étoiles* in Quebec in 2008 by Éditions Alto

Emblem is an imprint of McClelland & Stewart Ltd.
Emblem and colophon are registered trademarks of McClelland & Stewart Ltd.

LIBRARY AND ARCHIVES CANADA CATALOGUING IN PUBLICATION

Fortier, Dominique, 1972-
[Du bon usage des étoiles. English]
    On the proper use of stars / Dominique Fortier ; translated by Sheila Fischman.

Translation of: *Du bon usage des étoiles*.
ISBN 978-0-7710-4762-6

    1. Franklin, John, Sir, 1786-1847 – Fiction. 2. Franklin, Jane Lady, 1792-1875 – Fiction. 3. Crozier, Francis Rawdon Moira, 1796-1848 – Fiction. I. Fischman, Sheila II. Title. III. Title: Du bon usage des étoiles. English.

PS8611.O7733D813 2011   C843'.6   C2011-902026-2

We acknowledge the financial support of the Government of Canada through the Book Publishing Industry Development Program and that of the Government of Ontario through the Ontario Media Development Corporation's Ontario Book Initiative. We further acknowledge the support of the Canada Council for the Arts, which last year invested $20.1 million in writing and publishing throughout Canada, and the Ontario Arts Council for our publishing program.

 Canada Council Conseil des Arts
for the Arts   du Canada

We acknowledge the financial support of the Government of Canada, through the National Translation Program for Book Publishing, for our translation activities.

 ANCIENT FOREST
FRIENDLY

This book is printed on acid-free paper that is 100% ancient-forest friendly (40% post-consumer waste).

Typeset in Fournier by M&S, Toronto
Printed and bound in Canada

McClelland & Stewart Ltd.
75 Sherbourne Street
Toronto, Ontario
M5A 2P9
www.mcclelland.com

1 2 3 4 5   15 14 13 12 11

On the
PROPER USE
of STARS

Sail, sail adventurous Barks! Go fearless forth,
Storm on his glacier-seat the misty North,
Give to mankind the inhospitable zone,
And Britain's trident plant in seas unknown.

— Eleanor Porden

The Lords Commissioners of the Admiralty have, in every
respect, provided most liberally for the comforts of the
officers and men of an expedition which may, with the
facilities of the screw-propeller, and other advantages of
modern science, be attended with great results.

— *The Times*, May 12th, 1845

You are mad and I am blind;
Tell me, who will take us home?

— Jalal Ud Din Rumi

It was long disputed among the learned, whether the waters of the ocean are capable of being congealed; and many frivolous and absurd arguments, of course, were advanced to prove the impossibility of the fact. But the question is now completely resolved; and the freezing point of sea-water is established both by observation and experiment. To congeal such water of the ordinary saltiness, or containing nearly the thirtieth part of its weight of saline matter, it requires not an extreme cold: this process taking effect at about the 27th degree on the Fahrenheit scale, or only five degrees below the freezing point of fresh water.

Let us be wary, though, of arriving at a hasty conclusion regarding the phenomenon, as several have been tempted to do, that a Polar sea free of ice could not exist. On the contrary, a multitude of facts attest to the presence of such an expanse of water at the North Pole, of which we shall limit ourselves to citing the most obvious and most indisputable: as it is generally admitted that ice forms only in proximity to the coast, whether it be the mainland or islands, and that no such lands are to be found either at the Pole or thereabouts; as the Arctic sun shines for some twenty hours a day during the summer, which is quite sufficient to melt any icefield that may have formed during the winter months; as a good many ships have been able to sail in open water at elevated latitudes while their progress was impeded by icebergs, growlers, and floating ice at latitudes far more southern, one may only conclude that the North Pole is in all seasons surrounded by a sea that is utterly free of ice and, consequently, easily navigable.

Argo Navis

THE SUN WAS SHINING on that 19th day of May in 1845 when the *Erebus* and the *Terror* were preparing to cast off at Greenhithe, their reflections shivering on the greenish water of the port where floated garlands, handfuls of rice, and small dead fish. A crowd of a good ten thousand was assembled on the docks to witness the departure of Sir John Franklin, hero of the Arctic, who was setting off once again to conquer the mythic Northwest Passage, as always for the greater glory of the Empire. On the deck of the *Erebus*, in full regalia, the explorer was holding aloft a coloured handkerchief so that his wife Jane, Lady Franklin, could easily make him out in the midst of his inferiors, who were waving handkerchiefs of black silk. A brass band struck up the first bars of "God Save the Queen," the chords joining the cheers and farewells; emotion was nearly at its peak. One might have thought, as a shrewd observer noted in the newspaper the following day, that England was celebrating the explorer's triumphant return, not his departure. A dove flew lazily across the sky and touched down on the mast of the *Terror*, observing all the agitation with its head tipped a little to one side before settling comfortably, as if to hatch an egg. All agreed that it was a good omen.

Then the ships lumbered off to tackle unknown seas. The spectators went home. The hero of the Arctic, who was having difficulty recovering from a nasty bout of influenza, descended to his cabin, where he sipped a little tea and before long dozed off. Soon sailors, aides, and officers from the two ships returned to their respective posts. On the deck of the *Terror*, Francis Crozier, second-in-command of the expedition and commander of the ship, stood alone, looking back at the V-shaped wake left in the water. Hearing a muffled sound behind him on the deck, he turned around and nearly stepped on the dove, which had tumbled from the mast. He took one wing between his thumb and forefinger: still warm, the limp bird stared at him with its round eyes. Quite unceremoniously Crozier flung the creature into the sea. The surgeon's dog, Neptune, a rather ungainly mixture of beagle and wolfhound, pretended for a moment that he wanted to dive in after the bird, but changed his mind and proceeded instead to circle three times before he lay down on the deck and let out a loud fart.

25 May 1845

SCARCELY ONE WEEK has gone by since we weighed anchor, and the country that I left seems now to be farther away than the Moon and the stars above our heads, ever the same and ever different.

The sea is calm and the ships are sound. The *Terror* is my oldest friend, perhaps my only friend on this voyage when I cannot count on the presence of Ross, with whom I crossed the boundaries of Antarctica and into whose hands I would have agreed without hesitation to place my life once more. I insisted in vain that we have on board some of those whalers who know the treacherous waters of the Arctic better than any lieutenant of the British Navy, brave men to whom we owe most of the discoveries of this land of ice. Alas, the crew put together by Fitzjames is in the image of the man who chose it: elegant, enthusiastic, sure of itself, but sorely lacking in experience. Of the twenty-one officers – in the exclusive service of whom there are no fewer than eight men who I hope will not balk when the time comes that they must pull off their white gloves to scrub the deck or to furl the sails – only Sir John, the two ice masters, and I myself have ventured before into one or the other of the Polar circles. The most curious know nothing of the Arctic, may God have mercy upon us, save what they have read in the accounts of Parry and of Franklin himself, of which they recite passages with the same fervour as if they were verses of the Gospels. They are excited, like schoolboys being taken to the circus.

Scarcely one week and three times I have been summoned to dine on board the *Erebus*, Sir John seeming to believe that his duties include planning exquisite suppers and seeing to it that his officers do not suffer from boredom. In the morning he has brought to me small cards upon which it is written in careful script that "Sir John Franklin, Captain of the *Erebus*, requests the honour of the presence at his table of Francis Crozier, Captain of the *Terror*" — as if I were likely to confuse him with the captain of another vessel and present myself mistakenly on a ship where I was not expected. The men who are to bring him my reply wait, soaking wet, apparently astounded at such elaborate courtesies, while I turn the card over to write my answer, following which they row back in order to deliver the precious bit of paper. I must recommend that the lookouts agree upon a code so as to avoid these jaunts that transform our seamen pointlessly into messenger boys.

One dines well on the *Erebus*. Five bullocks that accompanied us on board the *Baretto Junior*, the supply ship, were sacrificed in a veritable hecatomb and prepared in various fashions. Yesterday we had a sole meunière, a splendid rib roast with buttered carrots and potatoes, and custard with berries, all served on silver plates struck with the arms or the monogram of the owner. The ridiculous is not pushed to the point of requiring that I supply my own cutlery, but I do use that of Sir John, who has apparently brought more than is strictly necessary.

We converse cheerfully about the voyage that is beginning, as if it were a hunting expedition with hounds, though I doubt that most of these gentlemen have ever killed any game more formidable than a partridge or, possibly, a fox. Most, like

DesVoeux, harbour a boundless admiration for Sir John, *hero of the Arctic*, whose accounts of his courageous deeds had marked their childhood, *the man who ate his boots* and, contrary to all expectations, had been able to survive on his own in a wild and hostile place.

At the sight of this happy gathering, of the valets who serve and take away the dishes under their silver lids, of the wines that accompany each new course, one might think he was at a supper at the country home of a gentleman whose livestock had experienced a particularly productive year or who had just married off his daughter. Except that there is no lady present – although it is true that they must withdraw in any case once the last bit of food has been swallowed, to leave the gentlemen to their cigars and port – and the candelabra are fixed firmly to the table, where there are silver goblets in place of crystal stemware. Without forgetting of course that once the merrymaking is over, rather than requesting that my carriage be brought, I ask for oarsmen to be called who, at the end of a voyage that can require as much as two hours on the rollers of the Atlantic, will take me back to the *Terror*, which I think of as the only home I've ever had.

4 June 1845

This morning, I discovered that my private stock of tobacco and tea, which I thought had never been delivered, had rather been taken on board the *Erebus*, to the cabin of Fitzjames, who I know has no reason to reproach himself since he has been trumpeting without interruption that some unknown friend has seen fit to give him an unexpected present on the occasion of his departure. I would be happy to disabuse him but it would be utterly absurd to split hairs like a fishwife over a few pounds of tea. I have suffered enough ridicule at the hands of Fitzjames, most often unbeknownst to him and without his having sought it, which only renders the insult more bitter. Fortnum and Mason, though, made no mistake as to the cabin to which their bill should be delivered. I paid without a second look at the provisions of that scoundrel who still has no idea about it and is quite certain it is a gift from an admirer – or, more likely, an appreciative lady.

I fear that the mood on board the *Terror* is not so euphoric as that on the *Erebus,* where, if I can rely on what I have been told, "laughter can be heard from morning to night." I confess that I have not yet had the pleasure of witnessing such a thing on board a ship, but who knows, perhaps Sir John possesses unsuspected talents as an entertainer. Unless the jubilation can be attributed to Fitzjames, whose countenance radiates joy and confidence.

My vessel may not ring out with laughter all day long, but I am nonetheless quite satisfied with the officers whose task it is to assist me, who appear to have similar feelings.

Edward Little, my lieutenant, is a serious man, although he has not much experience. He is less than forthcoming and neither of us finds it necessary to fill our silences with pointless chatter. He strikes me as level-headed and thoughtful and he knows how to appear firm while manifesting neither scorn nor contempt towards the men. Moreover, he does not attempt to make friends – a temptation to which I saw Fitzjames give in as early as the day after our departure, when he strolled among the sailors on the *Erebus*, offering them tobacco (*my* tobacco!) in addition to their daily ration – and knows that it is better to be respected than loved or feared.

John Peddie and Alexander MacDonald, surgeon and surgeon's assistant, form a curious pair, the second being as long and thin as the first is short and stocky; they resemble illustrations of Don Quixote of La Mancha and his faithful Sancho Panza, but reversed in a sense, because in this case it is the portly Sancho who instructs the lean, ingenious hidalgo. Those instructions are moreover few in number, for the assistant obviously knows what he is doing and does not need to be recalled to order. Every day he makes the rounds to inquire about the health of the men, recording in a small notebook various observations which he will then discuss with Peddie, without to date feeling the need to advise me of the fruit of these conversations. From this I deduce that everyone is in good health. As for Peddie, he spends most of his time in his cabin, where he has set up a tiny laboratory cluttered with flasks and vials that seem to me far too fragile to survive a voyage like the one on which we are setting out. There he mixes powders and liquids in order, he informed me, to produce sovereign remedies, known only to him, for scurvy and headache among others. These concoctions will enrich the well-stocked dispensary that he assembled before our departure and which contains – in addition to opium, laudanum, and morphine used to treat pain, camphor and cocaine reputed as stimulants, inoffensive castor oil and tincture of lobelia, all of them remedies commonly found on board ships about to undertake lengthy expeditions – substances of which I knew nothing, notably calomel and mandrake, which possess properties that, while not well known, yet allow us to foresee, he says, numerous uses. He feels a genuine passion for botany and is eager to begin putting together a herbarium of Arctic simples. I advised him that he was liable to be disappointed since it is likely that we shall arrive in Lancaster Sound at the moment when all vegetation disappears, but he assures me that one need only know how to look in order to find life where an untrained eye would see only barrenness. But let us not forget, he has never journeyed north of the sixtieth parallel.

7 June 1845

We are making good progress. What more is there to say save that every minute that takes me farther from her makes me suffer.

Supper on board the *Erebus* again, and this evening it required more than an hour to get there and the same to return once the coffee, the port, and the brandy had been duly ingested. The sea having swelled during the meal, the oarsmen had to redouble their efforts to have us arrive safe and sound, and we were all soaking wet from head to toe and shivering when we boarded the *Terror* again. I ordered them served a hot toddy, which seemed to restore their tranquility. It will take more to calm me.

The conversation was at first centred on various matters of little importance: the politics of the land recently enough departed that one still feels mysteriously tied to it; mutual acquaintances about whom we hadn't yet finished sharing news, news which will probably be repeated *ad infinitum* over the next two years whenever we feel nostalgic, embellished, depending on one's mood, with new details real or invented, until one can no longer distinguish the former from the latter. Then we broach subjects of interest to everyone, about which each of us has something to say: electricity, magnetism, and, more prosaically, the improvements made to the two ships that will allow them to spend several winters in Arctic waters treacherously sown with icebergs, where stray chunks of pack ice come in the morning to impede the passage that was clear the night before.

Sir John lists these technical wonders tirelessly, just as he would admire the coat of a horse or the inlay work of a writing desk. "Thanks to our central heating," he is fond of repeating, "the coal that fuels our boilers will serve a double purpose and we shall be as cozy as in the most modern houses on Park Lane."

"I was able to see the boilers when the locomotive engines they power were being installed in the holds," DesVoeux intervened. "Imagine, if they were able to pull dozens of cars, how they will laugh at the ice that aspires to stop them."

"At the Polar circle, the ice is sometimes several dozen feet thick," I pointed out, having often observed it. "Twelve locomotives would not suffice to break it in those places and it could crush the hull of a ship as easily as you would crush an eggshell in your hand."

Sir John looks at me for a moment without replying, as if I

have been intentionally offensive towards him or have deliberately shown a lack of respect. Then he starts again, in a tone that has lost none of its enthusiasm: "The reason for the prow of the *Terror* and that of the *Erebus* to be reinforced with tempered steel. With your knowledge of glacial waters, my dear Crozier, we shall find an anchorage where there is no risk of being in the way of those formidable pieces of ice."

And he raises his glass in a good-natured manner which may well mean that he forgives us both, the pack ice and me, for being such spoilsports.

10 June 1845

While we continue our crossing of the Atlantic, surprisingly calm for the time of year, I remember those sailors of yesterday, terrified at the thought of one day reaching the end of the Earth and falling into space, who nevertheless ventured into uncharted waters, driven by the same thirst for discovery that has tormented human beings from the dawn of time, some need to brave the unknown, to shed light on the mystery of that which rudely escapes man's understanding or his control, a desire to which every science, every religion, aims to respond.

As for me, I have gone to the end of the Earth, I have fallen into that void where there are no sea monsters or giant octopuses or mermaids or even God. I have found only night in that abyss, and of all the discoveries one can make, that is without a doubt the most dreadful.

TERROR *and* EREBUS *weighed anchor in the Port of Greenhithe on 20 May for a Journey undertaken by order of the Admiralty with the objective of discovering and navigating a Passage leading from the Atlantic Ocean to the Pacific. 129 men on board 2 Ships. The pages that follow are the Ship's Log of Captain Sir John Franklin, Commander in Chief of the Expedition.*

Satisfied, Sir John reread what he had just written with little concern for spelling or grammar, which had always rather bored him, but using his finest handwriting. It seemed to him an entirely fitting introduction which compared favourably with those of the accounts by Parry, Ross, and all the other explorers who had, alas, failed where he had every intention of succeeding. He regretted a little of course having waited so long before taking pen in hand, but he had been far too busy, and besides, except for their spectacular departure, nothing had yet occurred that warranted being recorded.

He had discussed at length with his wife the contents of this logbook, which would in all likelihood become a valuable document for geographers, seamen, merchants, servicemen, and scientists of the day, as well as for posterity. He had agreed with Lady Jane that he would use a concise style and content himself with delivering factual information as precisely as possible. As she had judiciously pointed out, it was best to limit oneself to the essential without striving for effect: accounts of explorations were too often embellished with inappropriate poetry that, far from enhancing the contents, could give rise to manifold interpretations – and this, she had pointed out, in matters of navigation was liable to end in disaster. In any event, once he was home, Lady Jane would take what he had written and polish it sentence by sentence, as she was accustomed to doing for all the documents her husband composed, and, with his consent, she would breathe new life into them and give them the scope by which one can recognize the accounts by the great discoverers. She had advised Sir John to encourage his men to keep logbooks as well and to collect them when the expedition returned in order to use them to enrich his own, a technique he had used when writing his half of *Two Voyages Undertaken by Order of the British Government, One by Land Directed by Captain Franklin; the Other by Sea Directed by Captain Parry, for the discovery of a Passage from the Atlantic Ocean into the Pacific Sea,* which had created such a stir.

While Sir John was rereading for the second time the words he had written, he sneezed, creating a small ink blot on the page. He considered retranscribing his entry on a new sheet of paper but thought to himself that one could not, dash it, expect that a journal written on the high seas, under conditions that were frequently difficult, indeed often beset by fearsome weather, be as clean as a letter composed quietly at home with one's feet before the hearth. He set down his pen and cracked his knuckles.

—

SHORTLY AFTER SIR JOHN's departure, Jane in turn set off for France. She was accompanied by her stooped and ancient father, her favourite sister, Fanny, her niece Sophia, and her stepdaughter Eleanor, who the doctors had assured them would benefit from a warm, dry climate. The young woman's health did not seem to improve, however, although on some days Lady Jane attributed Eleanor's various ailments to neurasthenia or to a far too phlegmatic nature rather than to a genuine weakness of constitution. She encouraged Eleanor to follow her own example of walking briskly, forced her to bathe in the icy sea at dawn, imposed a diet of raw red meat – only to note that none of it produced the slightest result. From that time on, her resources momentarily exhausted and her interest blunted, Lady Jane dropped the matter and contented herself with transporting her stepdaughter as if she were a burdensome suitcase from place to place according to the doctor's vague recommendations.

Generally she left her father and Eleanor at the hotel, where they indulged in sessions of reading and strolls in the neighbourhood that brought them back in time for lunch. Jane would set off at dawn in the company of a delighted Sophia and a clearly less enthusiastic Fanny. The three women, wearing elegant dresses and petticoats but shod in sturdy walking shoes and having exchanged their parasols for hikers' staffs, surveyed the bay of Mont Saint-Michel where the tide advanced "more rapidly than a galloping horse," crisscrossed the parks abounding in game that surrounded the Château de Chambord, investigated the fortifications of Carcassonne, and explored the celebrated ochre cliffs of Roussillon, from where Sophia brought home paints that, on canvas, would remind her for years of this delightful journey. True to her habit, Jane took with her everywhere a notebook in which she noted methodically the atmospheric conditions, the geographical location of the building, or the natural phenomenon on the day's itinerary as well as the reflections that her visit had inspired.

These ladies would come back at the end of the day, sometimes well into the evening, and over dinner with Eleanor and Mr. Griffin tell the sedentary pair about the wonders they had discovered.

One evening in Perpignan, an American who heard them conversing in English stood up from the table where he was dining alone and came over to introduce himself: Mr. Simonton was an industrialist from New England who had come to France to purchase works of art that would adorn the walls of the home he was having built for his young wife in Rhode Island. When Mr. Griffin introduced the elder of his daughters, the American, filled with interest, inquired: "Franklin, you say? Would you be related to the late Benjamin Franklin, my illustrious compatriot, of whose exploits you are no doubt aware?"

Vexed for several reasons, not the least of which being the fact that at the mention of the name *Franklin* anyone would think first of an American man of the people – even if he was a brilliant inventor – rather than of her explorer husband, Lady Jane replied curtly that she did not have that honour, and ignored the continuing interrogations of the American, who soon let the matter drop and set about quite brazenly courting Fanny and Sophia.

The travellers left France shortly afterwards, Mr. Griffin to return to England accompanied by Eleanor, who would spend the next few months with her grandparents, and Jane, Fanny, and Sophia for Portugal, where Lady Franklin was curious to visit some Gothic monasteries about which she had read a great deal.

One evening, exhausted by the day's excursions and feeling suspended between wakefulness and sleep, the memory of an insignificant incident came back to her. It was late one afternoon, a few days before Sir John's departure. Through the windows came swords of light that traced oblique lines on the Persian carpet. The parlour was sunk in shadowy light, a fire burned in the hearth, the room was bathed in the warmth of the dying day and the aroma of jasmine tea. Sitting at her marquetry writing desk, Lady Jane was busy striking out with a confident hand various items on a list that was several pages long. Sir John was slumped on a sofa, eyes closed, legs apart, mouth open. He was snoring faintly, now and then uttering some incoherent words or shivering briefly. A hot water bottle lay at his feet, where Athena, the cat, was cozily settled.

Alice, the middle-aged servant who had been in the service of Lady Jane's father and had come with her after her marriage, entered the room, carrying a set of meticulously polished silver cutlery. Lady Jane examined the pieces one by one, peering at her image in the blades of the knives, gazing briefly at the inverted reflection of the room in a spoon, then pointing to a wooden box already three-quarters filled with various personal effects that her husband would take on board the *Erebus*; as it was out of the question to use glass or china, the officers were required to supply their own cutlery and dishes if they did not wish to eat from wooden bowls. Obviously Jane had not chosen the costliest silverware for this voyage to the North Pole, but neither did she want her husband to present a sorry figure to his officers, some of whom came from excellent families. He would then take not the holiday silverware but the Sunday set, embellished with the head of a fish crowned with a garland of leaves and struck with his monogram, which was beginning to wear away on some of the most frequently used pieces.

After consulting her list one last time, she went to sit beside Sir John, who half wakened and muttered something before sinking back into a restless sleep. He was pale, his brow was damp, and he appeared to be cold. Jane considered for a moment the hot water bottle on which Athena was basking, then, changing her mind, picked up a flag of England embroidered with her husband's initials which lay neatly folded in the box that held the silverware. Careful not to waken Sir John, she draped him from shoulders to ankles with the Union Jack, which rose and fell as it followed the rhythm of his wheezy breathing.

Almost at once the cat got up lazily and with one supple leap crossed the carpet into the chest where the silver had been placed, setting off metallic thundering. Sir John woke with a start and, finding his movements impeded by the flag he had been wrapped in, tried for a moment to shake it off, not knowing what it was, like a butterfly awkwardly struggling to spread the threads of the cocoon that holds him prisoner. Then, finally realizing what the envelope was that was interfering with his movements, he let out a feeble cry and whispered to his wife:

"Ah, wretched woman! Do you not know what it is that we wrap in flags at sea?"

She showed little emotion, merely folded the Union Jack and, as Alice was coming in with a pile of books, asked for the lamps to be lit, for the sun had vanished and the parlour was filling with shadows.

Alone in an unfamiliar room, seeing the scene again almost as a dream, Lady Jane felt an inexplicable uneasiness.

24 June 1845

FOR THE FIRST TIME in these thirty-five years when I have spent
the better part of my time on the water, returning to land only
to take on fresh supplies before weighing anchor once more,
and as quickly as possible, it seems to me that this departure has
something absolute about it. I am not leaving *towards* something
as I have done so many times before, heart pounding, mind
inflamed at the thought of discovering a part of our world that
no one else has ever seen. I am now leaving something. I am
leaving Sophia, whom I wished to be my wife, my home, my
country, and who I know will never be mine just as I know
that she will always refuse that I be hers. I am setting sail towards
nothing, I am running away, quite simply. I do not know the
true objective of my voyage, since for me it is not so much
a matter of discovering the Northwest Passage, to which for
dozens of years others have attached so much importance, as
of returning home after having discovered it, holder of a secret
that will no longer be one. I have no one to whom to offer my
success, the way Neptune sets down at our feet the remains of
some seabird too puny or too badly damaged to be salted and
that the dog imagines he has hunted. What good is it to return
a hero if she only has eyes for another?

The day before yesterday we spotted our first icebergs, and today we are surrounded by them on all sides as if by some enchantment. One does not grow accustomed to such a landscape. The mountains of ice that shimmer with a mineral blue, green, turquoise rise up towards the sky like cathedrals built of snow. These masses, which make our ships seem Lilliputian by comparison, have in the sun a brilliance that is nearly supernatural: they seem to have emerged from a painting that depicts the surface of some unknown planet – or from the dream of a madman. They are, however, as dangerous as they are magnificent for, like men, they have the distinctive feature of concealing in their invisible depths the greater part of themselves, and one must navigate around these icy giants very slowly and very cautiously. The mist, which has not lifted for two days, makes navigation yet more difficult by wrapping those silent titans in a white and ghostly shroud.

In the open sea a pod of whales, at least six or seven, form a distant escort for the ships. One or two sometimes come close enough that we can see a burst of vapour shoot up, accompanied by a fantastic hissing sound. Every now and then they offer us the sight of their fan-shaped tails standing out against the horizon for a moment like vast black wings before they slap down, sending up showers of water.

We are well and truly in the Arctic.

We left the *Baretto Junior* behind on July 12, after the men entrusted to its captain the final letters for their wives, their fiancées, their families. I for my part addressed a brief missive to Ross in which I tried to be not too boring, though I could not prevent myself from telling him once more how much I would have preferred to serve under his orders rather than those of Sir John. Ever the optimist, the explorer had recommended that the captain advise families to address their correspondence to Petropavlosk on the Russian peninsula of Kamchatka, promising that he would come to pick it up on the other side of the Passage. Since that date, we have not seen a soul aside from the crews of the *Prince of Wales* and the *Enterprise,* two whaling vessels that appeared when the men were shooting down hundreds of seabirds. The flesh is tough, but once it has been salted, it will provide a change from Master Goldner's tinned beef and pork.

It has been reported that Sir John had been pleased to show the *Terror* to Captain Robert Martin, the master of one of those whaling vessels, who it appears marvelled at the ingenuity of the ship's engines. I was also told, but know not if I should believe it, that Franklin assured him we were carrying rations enough for five years and that we could make our supplies last as long as seven years should it be necessary.

However crude this exaggeration was (supposing that it had indeed been uttered), at the rate we are going we shall be home long before our supplies are exhausted. It took us only one month to cross Baffin Bay, after which, in keeping with the orders of Sir John Barrow, we sailed back up Lancaster Sound following the route taken by Parry, to reach the open Polar sea. Unable as we were to continue beyond Cape Walker because of the ice, we headed north towards the Wellington Channel until the pack ice again blocked our way. We nonetheless reached 77 degrees latitude north in a matter of months, which is no mean feat. I must admit that my fears regarding Sir John's competence were perhaps unfounded; all the members of the crew have truly grown attached to him and he has to date guided us very well.

Morale is still very high; one would swear that we were making ready to return to port, our mission already accomplished.

Instructions from Sir John Barrow
to Sir John Franklin

On putting to sea, you are to proceed, in the first place, by such a route as, from the wind and weather, you may deem to be the most suitable for despatch, to Davis' Strait, taking the transport with you to such a distance up that strait as you may be able to proceed without impediment from ice, being careful not to risk that vessel by allowing her to be beset in the ice or exposed to any violent contact with it. You will then avail yourself of the earliest opportunity of clearing the transport of the provisions and stores with which she is charged for the use of the expedition and you are then to send her back to England, giving to the agent or master such directions for his guidance as may appear to you most proper, and reporting by that opportunity your proceedings to our secretary for our information. You will then proceed in the execution of your orders into Baffin's Bay, and get as soon as possible to the western side of the strait, provided it should appear to you that the ice chiefly prevails on the eastern side or near the middle, the object being to enter Lancaster Sound with as little delay as possible. But as no specific directions can be given owing to the position of the ice varying from year to year, you will, of course, be guided by your own observations as to the course most eligible to be taken, in order to ensure a speedy arrival in the sound above mentioned. As, however, we have thought fit to cause each ship to be fitted with a small steam engine and propeller, to be used only in pushing the ships through channels between masses of ice when the wind is adverse, or in a calm, we trust the difficulty usually found in such cases will be much obviated. But as the supply of fuel to be taken in the ships is necessarily small, you will use it only in cases of difficulty.

Lancaster Sound and its continuation through Barrow's Strait having been four times navigated without any impediment, by Sir Edward Parry, and since frequently by whaling ships, will probably be found without any obstacles from ice or islands; and Sir Edward Parry having also proceeded from the latter in a straight course to Melville Island, and returned without experiencing any or very little difficulty; it is hoped that the remaining portion of the passage, about 900 miles, to Behring's Strait may also be found equally free from obstruction; and in proceeding to the westward, therefore, you will not stop to examine any openings either to the northward or southward in that strait, but continue to push to the westward without loss of time, in the latitude of about 74 ¼°, till you have reached the longitude of that portion of land on which Cape Walker is situated, or about 98° west. From that point we desire that every effort be used to endeavour to penetrate to the southward and westward in a course as direct towards Behring's Strait as the position and extent of the ice, or the existence of land, at present unknown, may admit.

. . .

You are well aware, having yourself been one of the intelligent travellers who have traversed the American shore of the Polar Sea, that the groups of islands that stretch from that shore to the northward to a distance not yet known, do not extend to the westward further than about the 120th degree of western longitude, and that beyond this, and to Behring's Strait, no land is visible from the American shore of the Polar Sea. In an undertaking of this description, much must be always left to the discretion of the commanding officer, and, as the objects of this expedition have been fully explained to you, and you have already had much experience on service of this nature, we are convinced we cannot do better than leave it to your judgment.

Sir John Barrow
Second Secretary to the Admiralty

20 August 1845

THE *Terror* AND THE *Erebus* have been sailing recently in virgin waters. We are advancing across a white map, drawing the landscape as if we were inventing it as we go, tracing as faithfully as possible the bays, coves, headlands, naming the mountains and the rivers as if we had been cast into the middle of a new Eden – though this one is icy, sterile, and for the most part uninhabited, but even so it is up to us to recognize and christen the territory. Before we came, the grandiose scenery of ice and sky did not exist; now we are tearing it from the nothingness to which it will never return, for henceforth it has a name. If ahead of us there is only empty space, the road we have travelled is riddled with observations, summaries, detailed information; it has joined the ever growing domain of what upon this Earth belongs to us.

3 September 1845

The icebergs that are slowly drifting out to the open sea form a changing setting the likes of which is unknown in England or anywhere else on terra firma, where the mountains do not move but remain sensibly where they are. What is paradoxical about this Arctic landscape is that we who look at it most often remain motionless, imprisoned by the ice, while it advances, backs up, unfurls, and is drawn tighter in a continual metamorphosis, as if it were in some mysterious way more alive than we are.

As I contemplate these fortresses of ice and snow, it strikes me as impossible not to be filled with a sense of one's own insignificance, not to know that one is minuscule and superfluous in the midst of so much wild and majestic beauty. It is difficult for me to find any echo of that feeling in the officers since they seem, for the most part, insensitive to the nature that surrounds us, of which they speak only as if it were some kind of particularly cunning animal that must be outwitted and caught. Today I cannot stop thinking that if there really is a hunter and a prey in this land of ice, it is we who are the quarry, pursued, trapped, at bay.

At last, it has happened. On this 9th day of September, 1845, we are iced in here in the open waters off Beechey Island, where we shall spend our first winter before continuing westward. The island is in fact merely a pile of rocks several miles long that is attached to Devon Island by a spit of pebbles and gravel. No tree grows there, nor any plant more than one inch high, nor does it provide shelter to any animal save the seabirds that land on it to dry off after fishing. It is a dreary and desolate place that seems to be mourning the absence of any life. In contrast, on board the two ships there reigns a peculiar frenzy, as if we had reached our goal, whereas it is still some months and thousands of miles away, should we indeed discover the Passage at the end of our hibernation. I must say that of the men around me, not one is familiar with the endless nights of the Polar circle – aside from Sir John, who is in good spirits after months at sea. Having departed gloomy and suffering from a cold, numb from years of the diplomat's life in Tasmania, he seems like a new man. He jokes with the men, proffers optimistic forecasts about the timetable we will follow and about the rewards that will be waiting for us on our return.

As for me, I would have been content to spend my life with Sophia, and if I thought that honour or money were liable to make her reconsider her decision, I would desire them with much more enthusiasm than they now inspire in me. Alas! No matter what she said, and although she maintained until the end that she would never be a sailor's wife, I have seen how she looked at Fitzjames. He is no less a sailor than I am, but on his head the cap is more elegant, on his shoulders the jacket is more becoming, and the colours of the navy give him the complexion of a fiancé. The one reward my heart has ever longed for will continue to elude me; whatever our success, and even if I should discover by myself a new continent to which would be given my name, Sophia would continue to have eyes only for Fitzjames's engaging smile.

— ADAM?

— Yes.

— Are you asleep?

— No.

— I'm cold.

— I know. Go to sleep, Thomas, you won't feel the cold.

— I'm wondering about something.

— Yes.

— D'you know what I'm wondering about?

— No.

— Why are the Moon and the Sun so much bigger here than in England? Do you know?

— No, I have no idea.

— Maybe it's because we're close to the end of the Earth here so we're closer to the Moon and the Sun.

— But the Earth is round . . .

— So?

— So, since it's round it doesn't have an end – either that, or any place on Earth could be an end, depending on where you are looking at it from.

— You mean that England could be the end of the Earth?

— Maybe.

— So?

— What, so?

— So why, when the Moon and the Sun touch the horizon, are they so big that you would swear that they're going to come crashing down and make a crater the size of Africa?

— I don't know. Maybe it's an illusion, a kind of mirage . . .

— What does that mean?

— It means that your eyes play tricks on you. Like when you see water standing out against the desert sand, for instance.

— If my eyes have decided to lie to me, I wish they'd show me a field of wheat rather than a giant Moon threatening to crash down onto Earth.

— Do you know what the Esquimaux James Ross met in Greenland thought?

— No, tell me.

— Well, they'd never seen white men before and they thought that he was a heavenly being. They asked him if he came from the Moon or from the Sun.

— And what did he say?

— I don't know. Probably that he came from the other side of the water.

— That's a lot harder to believe, isn't it?

The Sails

AT DAWN, IN THAT STATE which is no longer altogether part of the world of dream but is not yet wakefulness, Crozier sees again with astonishing precision a scene he lived through five months earlier and which now seemed to harbour some altogether crucial element.

It was two days before the departure of the expedition. Standing in the drizzle exuded by a grey and swollen sky, he was waiting for the arrival of Sir John, who was to come and make certain that the loading of foodstuffs and the final preparations were proceeding as they should.

Crozier had been standing on the wharf for more than half an hour when he spied Franklin, flanked by Lady Jane and – as he discovered in a blinding flash that tightened his chest so hard that he had trouble breathing – by Sophia Cracroft. She was escorted by an exuberant Fitzjames who seemed to be recounting some story to which she was listening with her head bowed slightly, apparently amused. Sophia was startled when she caught sight of Crozier but she quickly recovered and came up to him, her hand extended and smiling broadly, as if to show that she had nothing to hide, nothing to fear, no reason to be ashamed or ill at ease.

"Mr. Crozier, what a pleasant surprise," she murmured in a hushed voice. "But you must go inside, you'll catch your death of cold. As a matter of fact, my uncle has been suffering from a nasty influenza for some time now . . ."

As if to confirm her words, Sir John sneezed loudly, extracted a handkerchief from his pocket, and blew his nose with a sound like a trumpeting elephant. His wife, with a motherly touch, tightened the knot in the scarf around his neck.

" . . . and," Sophia went on, "who will command these vessels if you are both sick in bed?"

"I must see your uncle before noon. On an important matter. I knew that he was supposed to be here, but I was unaware that you . . ."

He broke off, unable to complete his thought, trying to express the rest of it by means of a vague movement that took in Sophia, Fitzjames, who was waiting politely a few steps away, and the sky from where, without let-up, diminutive icy drops that stabbed like needles were falling.

"Yes, we only decided at the last moment, in fact. My aunt chose to escort Sir John, who has a fever this morning, and James offered to show us around the machine room. One is told that it is very interesting."

"Indeed, indeed, most interesting," Crozier repeated almost without realizing it. *JAMES?* howled a voice inside him that was stronger than reason.

The men were bustling about, transporting dozens of crates on which could be read the word *tea*. Fitzjames asked Sophia if she knew the origin of the word. Despite himself, to break into this conversation that united them and to force the young woman to turn her eyes in his direction, Crozier replied that the word came from a Chinese ideogram whose exact name he could not recall. Then he stood there foolishly with his hands in his pockets.

"Ah, no, that's not it at all!" exclaimed Fitzjames. "As it happens, when tea began to arrive in Europe from the East Indies and China during the fifteenth century, nearly all of it was conveyed in transit via Lisbon, in Portugal. There, the stock meant for local consumption was taken away and on the other crates, those that were in transit, was drawn the letter *T*. Which gave in English *tea*, in French *thé*, in Spanish *té*, while in Portugal, where the crates were not marked with the word *transit*, one uses the word *cha*."

Sophia drank in his words. Crozier regretted having made himself ridiculous by putting forward an explanation of which he was not certain, even if he had trouble believing Fitzjames's story, which seemed to him far too fantastic. The younger man moved closer to Sophia, brushing her elbow and whispering:

"Dear lady, let us not stand here getting wet, let us board the ship, if you would be so kind, where you will be served one of the British Navy's celebrated hot toddies."

"Gladly," Sophia replied.

Then, turning to Crozier, she told him: "Don't stay too long in the rain, you're beginning to look like Mr. Darcy when he takes it into his head to dive into the duck pond . . ."

In the time it took him to realize that she was referring to one of Lady Jane's little dogs, she had disappeared in the wake of Fitzjames and her aunt, to whom the man had given his arm. Crozier stayed by himself with Sir John, who gave him an ill-tempered look.

"I say, to what do I owe this visit? What is so important that we must discuss it on a wharf in the rain?"

"Hmm . . . That is . . . Of course we can take shelter inside. I simply wanted to be certain that I would not miss you."

"Enough chattering," replied Sir John in the curt tone of voice he resorted to when he hoped to express efficiency but which was most often dictated by discomfort, cold, or hunger. "Let's get to the point. Speak up, Captain."

"It has to do with our rations, sir. I wanted to suggest that you avail yourself of a technique that was used by William Parry, among others, and yielded remarkable results."

"What are you talking about? For heaven's sake, man, speak clearly."

"Sprouted seeds."

"Pardon?"

"Sprouted seeds."

Thrusting his hand into the pocket of his greatcoat, Crozier took out a crumpled piece of towelling dotted with dozens of tiny, soft green heads, each attached to a small, pale-brown sheath.

"I know what sprouted seeds are, Crozier, thank you, I've seen vegetable gardens. But what the devil are these supposed to be used for?"

"Well, you see, sir, after six or eight months, when we will have consumed all our fresh fruit and vegetables, they could replace lettuce, spinach, and other greenery. They do not require soil or even light to grow. One need only place the seeds on a scrap of cloth, water them regularly, and in less than a week . . . *voila!* And on the ships where they have been cultivated, there has not been even one case of scurvy."

"But, but, but," Sir John broke in, like a teacher who has just been waiting for the right moment to catch out a dunce, "that is precisely why we are bringing I don't know many barrels of lemon juice —"

"If you will allow me, Sir John, the men don't care for lemon juice. I have often seen some of them pretend to swallow it, then spit it out right away."

"Never mind," said Sir John, who had started to sway from one foot to the other, a sign of growing impatience, "we shall distribute it to them the way that one administers medicine to a child, and if necessary we will ask them to open their mouths and stick out their tongues after they've swallowed it. And then most important of all, dear Crozier, you forget that we shall have with us hundreds of tins of preserved vegetables already cooked and seasoned and ready to be eaten. Between a mixture of diced potatoes, carrots, and peas and your four seeds, which will the men prefer, will you tell me?"

There was some truth to what he said. The tiny leaves on their slender stems, still prisoner of the seed that had served them as a cover, were not very tempting.

"And then," continued Sir John, who did not intend to have such a fine beginning interrupted, "do you not think that we shall have better things to do than play at being gardeners to your sprouts? No, Crozier, believe me, between geographical tracings, temperatures, magnetic readings, navigation as such, and the upkeep of the ships, I doubt very much that we'll have the time or the desire to keep up a vegetable garden, not even one the size of a handkerchief. It is precisely for that reason that these tinned foods are ideal: they eliminate even the need to prepare the foodstuffs, to cut them up and cook them – all lengthy and tedious procedures. One need only open them, heat up the contents, and there you go, ready to feed an army."

"No doubt, Sir John."

Crozier was well aware that the game was lost. Mechanically, he turned over and over in his fingers the soft green shoots. Then he realized that he had never sampled the contents of those tins that were being loaded on in their thousands.

"Have you tasted them, Sir John?"

"I beg your pardon?"

"Those tins of vegetables –"

"And meat!"

"Those tins of vegetables and meat that we are taking with us in such great quantity?"

"Good heavens, no, Crozier, I've eaten everything in my life when I've had to, from rock tripe to raw seal meat to bear steak and even the leather of my shoes, as you are not unaware, but I have never understood the purpose of submitting pointlessly to the exercise. I have consulted the lists of products offered by Mr. Goldner and I can assure you that they are far superior to the everyday fare served to the men during long voyages. But you need not worry: for the officers, the menu will be more traditional. We shall take on masses of salted meats and pickles of all sorts."

"I have no doubt where that is concerned, Sir John," Crozier replied.

"On that, with your permission, I shall go and dry off."

"Of course, Sir John, I thank you."

And Sir John lumbered off in the direction of the gangway leading to the deck of the *Terror*.

Crozier stopped the first sailor who went past him pulling a trolley, upon which were piled some twenty huge tins of food, and asked him to open one.

"Impossible, sir. These provisions are intended for the *Terror*, which is leaving in just a few days to spend a year in the Arctic. We're not allowed to open these tins for no reason."

"Do you know who I am?"

The sailor considered Crozier standing in front of him soaking wet from head to foot, his coat hanging forlornly from his broad shoulders, water dripping from his hair. Briefly, his face expressed doubt, but he had certainly seen pictures of Sir John Franklin. He knew that this man could not be him.

"No, sir."

Crozier sighed.

"Never mind."

He picked up the two tins from the top of the pile and with a wave dismissed the sailor, who left without further ado. Then, kneeling on the wet quay, Crozier took his knife from his pocket and started to open a tin on the label of which could be read: *Beef Stew*.

He had to start over twice before he could properly cut open the metal cylinder, from which came a sweetish smell. Crozier dipped his finger in the thick brown liquid where pieces of meat were floating, smelled it cautiously before touching it with his tongue, and immediately spat. Examining the stew more carefully, he discovered that it contained bits of meat that were half raw. He spilled the entire contents of the tin onto the quay and began to stir it with his knife under the watchful eye of the sailors who continued to follow one another, carrying rations. In the brownish mixture, which was being thinned by the rain, he discovered as well some bits of bone and something that looked very much like a piece of ear that someone had forgotten to relieve of its fur.

Crozier rose to his feet and ordered in a powerful voice: "Stop the loading!"

Dispatched to the premises to sort out the crisis, Fitzjames ordered that some twenty tins of various sizes containing meats, soups, and vegetables be opened. He did not go so far as to taste them but sniffed their contents and decreed that in nineteen cases it was altogether acceptable. As for the twentieth tin, from which came a smell of sulphur, well, nothing is perfect, and it was to be expected that a certain percentage would be lost. They started loading again a few hours later and finished during the night, while Crozier, unable to go home, paced the streets.

While he was walking in the rain, which had let up somewhat and was now only a drizzle, he went over again in his mind the scene he had been part of earlier that afternoon, as if he were trying to punish himself for some hope that was unseemly to maintain: the unexpected arrival of Sophia, his own idiotic, trite remarks, and Fitzjames's loquaciousness, his vaguely impertinent way of suggesting to the young woman "one of the British Navy's celebrated hot toddies." In the twenty years he had spent in the ranks of the aforementioned British Navy, where grog was concerned Crozier had never tasted anything that was liable to delight the taste buds of a young woman from polite society. Of course one was sometimes given under that name a mixture of rum, gin, and lemon juice, enlivened on a lucky day by a cube of sugar, but never would it have crossed his mind to offer the bitter brew – concocted notably to bring down a fever or to numb a sailor on whom a painful operation was about to be performed – as an exotic drink, and even less as a delicacy. Touching her red lips to it, Sophia would probably shudder as much from the bitterness of the drink as from the excitement she would feel at savouring it in the company of a handsome officer who would not hesitate to tell her the story of the pirates from whom the rum had been snatched in a hard-won victory.

Crozier knew how to lead men into battle as into peace, he knew how to read the sea and the landscape, the clouds and the stars. He knew the great wooden body of his ship as certainly as that of a faithful dog, but he did not and would never know how to offer a cup of lukewarm, sour liquid to a lady in such a way that she would find it delicious and consider herself obliged to him. For that, he would have been willing to trade all the rest.

29 November 1845

To pass the time, I have set out to be a teacher to anyone who might be interested in learning. This has brought together an ill-assorted group to whom every day I give lessons that DesVoeux does not look kindly upon – which, I must admit, adds to my satisfaction at playing schoolmaster. Among my pupils, there are some who signed their documents of engagement by scrawling awkward *X*s on the paper presented to them. Patiently, I draw large letters on a slate which the men, like children, try to copy, their tongues sticking out. As paper and ink are valued resources and the number of slates is limited, some carve the letters into pieces of wood taken from empty barrels that once held victuals, while others merely trace them in the air with their fingers, or onto the table in front of them.

This morning, DesVoeux came in while I was questioning one of them.

"Is this the way to write *Terror,* sir?"

DesVoeux answered before I could open my mouth: "No, imbecile, you've put two *R*s where it only takes one."

I looked at him, shocked, but he seemed serious. So the handsome dandy is illiterate. I should have suspected. Once he had turned his heels, looking smug, I explained to the men that as far as I was concerned, I would rather that we continued to write *Terror* with two *R*s.

Just then, the very names of the ships, familiar creatures whose slightest nooks and crannies I knew, struck me as an ill omen. Through what aberration, through what grim irony had a vessel that was making ready to spend months in total obscurity been given the name of the Greek god of darkness?

For two or three days the sun has shown itself for only a few minutes then disappeared on the horizon straightaway like a bird shot down in mid-flight. The thin bright disk heaves itself with difficulty above the white line that marks the meeting point of sky and Earth, stays there suspended for several seconds, nearly trembling, surrounded by a feeble halo of greyish light, then immediately plunges again after it has brushed against the snow for a moment, not to reappear until the following day, even more briefly.

7 January 1846

Today, scarcely six months after weighing anchor in the port of Greenhithe, we buried our second dead man. If it is true, as certain savage peoples maintain, that one is not at home in a land until one's dead have been entrusted to it, we are now bound forever to this inhospitable bit of island as I would never have chosen to be.

It took the better part of a day before we could dig in the frozen ground the grave wherein we laid the body of John Hartell. I must confess that when I was told of his demise it took several seconds before I could recollect his face. It gave rise to a feeling of shame. True, he was a member of the *Erebus* crew, but in the end those men are all under my responsibility as well as under Sir John's. I told myself that I would have been a mediocre father. What will I ever know of it?

It was a most sober service. The crews of the two ships gathered around the grave, Sir John read the 23rd Psalm in an unsteady voice before delivering a few words about Hartell, of whom he said that he was an excellent sailor, a courageous young man full of life. At that moment I could not help wondering if he had known who was meant when he was notified of the young man's death – indeed, if he knew now as he was offering his eulogy.

A few men were weeping silently under the grey sky. We observed a minute's silence in memory of the deceased, then we set about covering the body with stones, after which the men went back to their ships with a heavy tread. If henceforth this land to which we have given one of our men belongs to us, we belong to it as well.

John Torrington's grave was dug forty-eight hours later, to the right of the first. He had suffered from a persistent cough since our departure, a cough that was resistant to the treatments with camphor and eucalyptus lavished on him by MacDonald, who was concerned about seeing it spread through the crew, and that had worsened since we'd arrived at the Arctic Circle. Torrington had spent the past week confined to bed, and when I went to see him, he had the feverish eyes of one who sees death drawing near; he was holding a blood-stained handkerchief over his mouth.

I went myself to announce his passing to Sir John, who put his head in his hands and, for a long moment, said nothing. Then he asked me how old John Torrington was, and if he had a family in England. I knew, having asked the question of

Little a few hours earlier, that he was not married, but that his parents were still alive and that they were destitute. He ran his hands over his face and asked me if I thought that he could use the 23rd Psalm for the ceremony again, for he had not anticipated another. He added, as if it were self-evident, that he would hasten to remedy the situation. That remark caught me up short and I wondered for a second if he had lost his mind and imagined that he could bring the dead back to life, but soon I realized that he was instead offering to find a new passage that would be suitable for a burial service. I merely nodded and he did likewise. As I was leaving his cabin, I saw him consulting his Bible as if it were his most urgent duty. But who can say where lies the true duty of men, and who knows if the words that he may find there will be able to restore the serenity of those to whom he will read them . . .

There now stand upon Beechey Island two identical graves, two minute crosses under the immensity of the sky, on a desolate scrap of land that seems to have been intended from time immemorial to become a cemetery. It would be hard to say whether these flimsy sentinels are guarding the boats or defending the windswept island where they are planted.

23.1

The Lord is my shepherd; I shall not want.

23.2

He maketh me to lie down in green pastures: he leadeth me beside the still waters.

23.3

He restoreth my soul: he leadeth me in the paths of righteousness for his name's sake.

23.4

Yea, though I walk through the valley of the shadow of death, I will fear no evil: for thou art with me; thy rod and thy staff they comfort me.

23.5

Thou preparest a table before me in the presence of mine enemies: thou anointest my head with oil; my cup runneth over.

23.6

Surely goodness and mercy shall follow me all the days of my life: and I will dwell in the house of the Lord for ever.

ONCE THE PORTUGUESE monasteries had been inspected – a visit that inspired Lady Jane to compose a number of heartfelt pages on the relationship between Gothic architecture and light – the travellers headed for Madeira, and from there to the West Indies and then the United States. In New York and in Boston, as was her habit, Lady Jane missed neither a museum nor a natural or historic site, whether significant or of no consequence, and she visited as well a number of universities, libraries, even factories, hospitals, and prisons, covering with notes the small writing pads brought along for that purpose. She also used the opportunity to climb Mount Washington, in New Hampshire, an ascent of some 6,300 feet, which she accomplished alone, accompanied by a guide, while Sophia and Fanny, who did not share her passion for heights, treated themselves to less perilous strolls along the lake bordered with spruce trees where their hotel was nestled.

After that, Lady Jane took it into her head to go and meet her husband, whose ships would undoubtedly appear shortly on the west coast of America. For a few moments, she considered the possibility of embarking with Sophia (Fanny, exhausted, insisted on going back to England at once) on a vessel that would round Cape Horn before heading up towards California, but instead she chose the land route, which allowed her to follow the itinerary travelled by Alexander von Humboldt, an explorer of the sort that Lady Jane favoured: noble, well read, voluble, he shared his observations and hypotheses in accounts that were utterly clear, written in a style that was always brisk and nimble. If Lady Jane Franklin had allowed herself to imagine what man she might have dreamed of being, she would have been obliged to admit that she would not mind slipping into the skin, not of her rubicund spouse, but of the fiery von Humboldt. Thus this part of the voyage, which was said to be of legendary difficulty, took on a particular appeal from the fact that it corresponded – inaccurately, alas – to the route followed by von Humboldt and Aimé Bonpland. Crossing the isthmus of Panama was uneventful: clouds of midges pressed against the mosquito netting of their sedan chairs, but very few were in fact able to get inside. Lady Jane's epidermis was used to their bites, unlike Sophia's, which was covered with rose-colored swellings to which a series of a foul-smelling poultices had to be applied. Only once did she spy a scorpion, which one of the guides hastened to flatten with his foot, murmuring words that could have been an incantation; howler monkeys threw branches and fruits at them from the treetops, but she was never able to make out anything of those creatures save long elastic tails as they fled squawking through the leaves; and of the brigands feared, heralded, nearly hoped for, not a trace. She who had always refused to follow anyone at all now went nonetheless happily along the trail left almost fifty years before by a tremulous old man, working on his magnum opus, entitled simply *Kosmos*.

If the first stages of the journey were magnified by Lady Jane's intoxication at the thought of setting foot (most often metaphorically, for rarely did she feel the need to descend from her sedan chair, in which it was so easy to raise the curtains to admire the landscape) in the tracks left by the larger-than-life explorer who was, so to speak, showing her the road to follow, Lady Jane looked forward to the last leg with a genuine feeling of elation, for she had every hope of being reunited with her illustrious spouse, home from a triumphant expedition. She had even pictured herself rounding the fearsome Cape Horn on board the *Erebus*, which would take her across the Atlantic to return at Sir John's side to England, where she too would arrive as a conqueror. At the very least she was expecting to find on the West Coast some word about her husband, whom whalers or traders could not have failed to catch sight of in the Polar seas. But of the expedition of Her Majesty's Navy there was no news, and for the voyage home, Lady Jane, in the company of her niece, embarked upon a ship filled with dull businessmen, politicians, and a good many chilly old ladies.

Back at Bedford Place, making the best of it, she took up her London activities where she had left them. Along with the status of hero's wife went a certain number of absolute demands, not the least of which was to offer her visitors – whose numbers would multiply over the coming weeks – an interior at once beyond reproach and always surprising, implacably British in both spirit and nature, that would also evoke the adventure, even the heroism with which its occupants were familiar, a delicate balance that Lady Jane excelled at preserving thanks to a thousand and one connections, private as well as professional.

Among the latter, Mr. Thompson, whom Lady Jane and Sophia never called anything but Mr. T., was indisputably the most prominent tea merchant in London. This designation seemed far too common, though, to apply to such a refined individual, and he preferred to call himself a "broker in rare essences." It was said that he turned down more clients than he deigned to accept and that among the rejected – obviously displeased – were certain members of the royal family, condemned to sip the dull blends of Mister Twinings that had plagued their mothers and grandmothers before them. While she could not claim to be the wealthiest or the most highly born of Mr. T.'s clients, Lady Jane was nonetheless one of those he favoured, going so far as to present his elixirs himself. He enjoyed her curiosity and her enthusiasm for all things new and he marvelled at her knowledge of geography, anthropology, and botany, knowledge most surprising in a woman, even through she was the wife of the most celebrated explorer in the land. Of course, Sir John himself was part of Mr. T.'s interest in Lady Jane. Always on the lookout for novelties and rare articles, he had begged the famous captain to be so kind as to bring him samples of the small aromatic plant called "northern tea," whose leaves gave off the fragrance of mint, which the *coureurs de bois* chewed to freshen their breath and drank as a decoction for treating colic. For Mr. T. also liked to think of himself as a kind of herbalist, and while he placed tea well above all other plants, he did not look down on certain ones that had especially interesting properties. Sir John seemed to him then a fellow discoverer. It is true that the broker in rare essences, whose constitution was rather feeble, had never stepped onto the deck of a ship – nor, consequently, on foreign soil – but his emissaries brought to him, along with the silks, the medicinal plants, and the thousand and one varieties of tea that he offered to his pampered clientele, supplies of stories about the distant lands visited and their customs, so that he sometimes had the impression that he had personally surveyed Cathay or Bombay. When he proposed to the elegant London ladies the scented teas which he sold to them for a small fortune, he was close to believing that he, too, was taking part in the greatness of the Empire.

This morning he was especially pleased with the treasures he would reveal to Lady Jane. For in addition to the insipid Earl Grey – named for the former Prime Minister, who had been presented, by way of thanks for some favour or other, with the bergamot-scented leaves everyone was inexplicably infatuated with – and the delicate jasmine tea of which Lady Jane always kept a stock to quench the thirst of ladies whose palates were not adventurous, and which Mr. T. himself delivered in porcelain jars decorated with serpents and dragons, he had brought three boxes made of precious wood.

He opened the first with tremendous caution to reveal some grey-green leaves that gave off a sweet but strangely heady fragrance, somewhat reminiscent of the earth after rain and of the unopened buds of flowers.

"Allow me to introduce the white tea of Fujian, in the county of Zeng Huo in China. A splendid spot . . . Hills with steep sides and rounded summits that resemble kneeling giants trying to stand to touch the sky. This tea is harvested only a few days a year, at the beginning of May, by young virgins with a delicate touch. It is usually reserved exclusively for the imperial family."

"Mmm," noted Lady Jane as she breathed in the aroma from the box. "It seems to me that I sampled it at Lady Cheswick's. Could it have been you who sold it to her?"

"Certainly not," the merchant retorted, outraged that his marvel should be compared with some concoction or other. "I do not know where that lady purchases her supplies but I can assure you that this tea, a genuine nectar, is to be found on only four or five tables throughout the land."

"Yes," replied Lady Jane, who was in the habit of agreeing with the person with whom she was speaking, even when they thought that they were in the middle of an intense debate, as soon as the matter seemed to her to have been resolved or no longer interested her, as was rather frequently the case. "But I find it a little . . . a little bland. Show me what else you have."

Mr. T. let the matter drop. With much ceremony, he set the first box down beside him and opened the second, which contained leaves of a more assertive green and gave off an intense vegetal aroma.

"This is the Yun Wu, a green tea from the province of Jiangxi. Its name means *cloud and mist*. It was picked at the top of Mount Lu, which has nearly impenetrable slopes and a peak that is constantly draped in rolls of mist. As the old Chinese proverb has it, where there are clouds and fog we are assured of finding good tea. Its leaves are then dried in the sun without being subjected to any form of fermentation, which enables them to conserve their perfume intact. Allow me . . ."

He pinched a few leaves between his thumb and forefinger and dropped them into a small, squat cup without a handle, then poured in some water. The plant-like aroma became more pronounced, as if a miniature swamp were coming to life and exuding delicate scrolls of steam. Mr. T. breathed in delightedly while Lady Jane drew back imperceptibly in her chair. Something about this tea was not altogether proper; it seemed to her oddly indecent. The merchant insisted she admire the rich jade-green hue.

"This nectar has been enjoyed by the imperial court since the Song dynasty," he pointed out. "Do smell."

Overcoming her reluctance, Lady Jane stretched out her neck, inhaled once. The powerful, nearly musky aroma provoked a hiccup which she suppressed as best she could. Taking out her handkerchief, she asked to be shown a black tea. Mr. T. sighed, then picked up the third box and opened it. From the contents came a spicy, perfumed aroma that was at once sweet and pungent.

"Oh!" she said, already won over. "What is this?"

"A unique blend from the East Indies that is called chai, a skilful assemblage of black teas to which have been added, in proportions kept secret for generations, pepper, cinnamon, star anise, ginger, cardamom, and other spices. It is generally drunk with hot milk and a good quantity of sugar. Let me give you some to taste."

He spooned the mixture of leaves and spices into a new cup, and ceremoniously added a little milk and two squares of sugar before presenting the drink to Lady Jane.

"I must warn you, Lady Jane, this is extremely strong. People have told me that it sometimes causes palpitations in ladies, and therefore is more appropriate for gentlemen, whose tastes it matches more closely."

Lady Jane was no longer listening. Eyes closed, she was savouring the exquisite infusion that scarcely pricked her tongue and warmed her throat delightfully.

"Dear Mr. Thompson, I should like to purchase your entire stock. Alice will pay you."

—

AT FIRST ONLY THREE or four sailors with nothing to do attended the lessons given in the common room, where Crozier had arranged some crates in a row as seats. Soon, however, the volunteers were more numerous. A big strapping fellow called Paterson, pressing Crozier not to make fun of him, asked to be taught to read. Another made it a point of honour to demonstrate that he could identify all the letters of the alphabet (a word that for some reason he pronounced *alphabeet*) but acknowledged that he did not know how to write them. Others were curious to learn the principles of physics, optics, the laws of astronomy and magnetism – subjects on which Crozier enjoyed holding forth. Others still spent those few hours consulting the technical and scientific works that had been brought on board in their hundreds. But oddly enough, it was the novels and books of poems that enjoyed the greatest success. These men, who had previously considered fiction to be a pastime that was good enough for entertaining women (unless it was putting pernicious ideas into the brains of young girls), were fighting over *The Vicar of Wakefield* and meditating on the poems of Lord Tennyson – one of whose virtues, and it was not the least, consisted in the fact that he was a nephew of Sir John. During those precious minutes when the lower decks were bathed in a pallid light, the corner of the usually cluttered and overpopulated room took on the appearance of a scriptorium.

One seaman showed an unexpected talent for calligraphy; another was able to solve equations with a number of unknowns without the help of pen and paper; a cook's helper discovered a passion for magnetism, a science for which he had something of a gift, as Crozier discovered when he was setting out the basic principles to a small group.

"And so the reason why a compass needle always points to the north is that is magnetized."

"Does it become magnetized or has it always been?"

"Some metals are naturally magnetized: iron, for instance, which was found in the vicinity of the city of Magnesia in Turkey, to which the phenomenon of magnetism owes its name. For a long time those were the metals used for making compasses. In more recent years, however, we have learned how to magnetize certain metals by heating and then chilling them," he replied, happy to see them showing an interest in such questions of orientation on which their survival might depend.

"But," interrupted the assistant cook, a fair-haired young fellow who could not have been more than eighteen, "does that mean the needle points towards the Pole because it is attracted there as if by a magnet? So that Earth herself serves as a magnet, is that right, sir?"

"You're absolutely correct." Crozier nodded, particularly satisfied to note that the general theory, while abstract and relatively complex, could be understood by even the most simple-minded.

"But sir," the young man went on, sounding troubled, "is it not true that magnetized metals are always attracted by the South Pole of the magnet, not the North?"

"What's he carrying on about?" others on all sides were asking.

At these words, Francis Rawdon Moira Crozier, who had

been made a Fellow of the Royal Society and of the Royal Astronomical Society because of the excellence and the significance of his work on magnetism, who had been closely involved in the discovery of the South Magnetic Pole before he identified the location of the North Magnetic Pole, was speechless.

The assistant cook's voice was now tinged with despair:

"If that is the case, then the North Pole is actually the South Pole of the magnet, the South Magnetic Pole, and the real North Magnetic Pole is in Antarctica, is that not true, sir?"

"Idiot!" whispered the man next to him, elbowing him in the ribs. "Do you think you're at the South Pole now? Isn't it cold enough for you? Or maybe you think you're in Australia with the Zulus?"

Crozier noticed neither the discourtesy nor the ethnological absurdity. He had felt the Earth open beneath his feet, the Earth he had travelled, whose continents and seas he had explored, surveyed, measured, mapped, but whose innermost laws were obviously still escaping him. How had he not thought about that? Of course it changed nothing: whether a pole was *called* North or South changed neither its location nor its functioning. But if he, along with generations of explorers and scientists, had been able to make such a crass error, how could he believe that he had not committed other equally tragic ones?

The assistant cook — only then did Crozier realize that he did not know the boy's name — was squatting on the crate that he was using as a seat. Motionless, with shoulders hunched and chin bent over his chest, he did not take his eyes off his commander, from whom he expected a denial, an explanation, a jibe. Quite obviously he hoped that the man standing in front of him, who was his superior in age, constitution, experience, and education, not to mention in rank and fortune, would set him straight; he wanted things to resume the places they'd always held.

But Crozier did not even think of scoffing, as he sometimes did when one of the men asked a question that was just too absurd. He confined himself to saying, his voice choked, that the lesson was over and dismissed his students without subjecting them, as he usually did, to a problem of mathematics or logic that would keep their minds busy until the following day. The assistant cook got to his feet with the others, his back still bent.

Crozier called to him: "I say!"

Several pairs of inquiring eyes rose.

"You!" he said, pointing to the young man, who sat down again, resigned.

When the others had gone, Crozier came and sat beside him.

"What is your name?"

"Adam, sir."

"Just Adam, or do you have a last name, too?"

"They call me Adam Tuesday, sir, because I was found one Tuesday on the steps of the orphanage. I guess that's my family name. It is the one I put down when I signed up, sir."

"Very well, Adam Tuesday, was it perhaps at the orphanage that you were taught about magnetism?"

"No, sir. I learned it here, from books in the library. I never saw so many, and they told me I could read them when my work was done," he added quickly, like a child expecting to be scolded.

"They told you the truth. Those books were brought on board for the benefit of everyone, and everyone may consult them as he wishes. Which ones did you read, then?"

"All of them, sir."

"You read every one of the books that deal with magnetism?"

"Yes, sir, and all the others, too. I particularly liked the *Sonnets* of William Shakespeare, sir."

12 January 1846

To WHILE AWAY the boredom of the long winter months, someone had the idea of reviving Parry's Royal Arctic Theatre as a way of entertaining our crew. The men devoted themselves to it with a fervour and good humour that showed how profoundly they long for something to do. They managed to persuade DesVoeux, who strikes me as a man who would not let pass an opportunity to show himself off to advantage, to play a small part in their farce. Perhaps I am being unfair. Perhaps he is only thinking about the men's morale and participates with good grace in their masquerade, the way an older brother will agree to briefly take part in his younger brother's games. As for me, I shall be content with the role of spectator – which does have its own importance, for it goes without saying that these antics have meaning only if someone is there to witness them.

For a week now the lessons have gone from two and a half hours to one hour per day. The time thereby freed is spent on rehearsals and endless whispered secret meetings. Every day, in one corner of the lower deck, a workshop is fitted out where a dozen men bustle about making costumes from old uniforms, blankets, and cloth, some brought specifically for the occasion. The men are silent and careful to hide any costume-making from my eyes and from those of anyone who is not one of the actors. In another corner sets are being assembled and painted with the help of onion skins and beet juice. Harvey, the cartographer, has let himself get caught up in it and I am rather curious to see the result.

Like DesVoeux, however, he refuses to expose the slightest detail, despite efforts by Fitzjames to worm some information out of him. The first and only performance by the troop, which has been christened Her Majesty's Northern Theatre, is to be presented in some ten days' time. I believe the story will be adapted from an old French play that has turned up in the library of the *Erebus* and which, it is said, made men laugh until they cried.

Journey to the Moon

A comedy in three acts presented by
Her Majesty's Northern Theatre

In order of appearance:

SAVINIEN CYRANO DE BERGERAC
FIRST FRIEND
SECOND FRIEND

ACT 1, SCENE 1

Night. Three tipsy friends are walking down a faintly lit street,
arguing. Above the rooftops the full moon is slowly rising.

FIRST FRIEND

See how round the moon is tonight!

SECOND FRIEND

You would swear it was a huge meringue pie. Hmmm . . . I
wouldn't say no to a slice! *(They laugh.)*

CYRANO

And, gentlemen, if that Moon were a world like this one, for
which our world served as Moon?

But of course. Why stop there? Why should our world not serve as its Sun, for heaven's sake! *(More laughter.)*

CYRANO

Laugh if you will. Who is to say that at this very moment people in some other Moon are not poking fun at a man who maintains that this globe is a world? Very well, good luck along the road.

(The friends separate, still laughing. The others go away. Cyrano goes home. We hear sounds of clinking glass, then he comes out carrying a dozen flasks filled with liquid.)

CYRANO *(speaking to himself while he stares at the flasks on his belt)*
Before this evening I knew not to what purpose I would put the dew taken from the petals of a thousand poppies, an operation which required that I rise before dawn over ten days so as to collect the precious liquid before it evaporated, irresistibly attracted by the Sun. As the day star has set, it stands to reason that this dew will be quite naturally attracted by the Moon, as will I.

(Once the operation is complete he uncorks the flasks one by one, rubs his hands and waits a few seconds. Then he rises, slowly, above the rooftops.)

ACT I, SCENE 2

CYRANO
SIX SELENES
DÆMON OF SOCRATES

An undulating, uniformly white landscape under a sky speckled with stars, where we make out a brown and green planet bigger than the others: Earth. Cyrano is stretched out on the ground, his flasks spread around him. He is coming back to himself.

CYRANO

Where am I? Oh, my head . . . I remember nothing. What has happened to me? *(Looking around him.)* But . . . Can it be that . . . Have I then arrived on . . .

(Enter a group of six Selenes, their only garment a kind of a long loincloth. Their skin and hair are white as flour and they seem highly irritated.)

SELENES *(pointing to Cyrano)*

Wooloo wooloo wooloo!

CYRANO

Would you gentlemen be so kind as to inform me in what country I now find myself? I set out from the city of Paris, I know not if it was several minutes ago or several hours, and I am now here among you . . .

SELENES *(more and more annoyed)*

WOOLOO WOOLOO WOOLOO!

(They approach Cyrano, help him to his feet, and surround him. One grabs his hat, another pulls his moustache.)

CYRANO

Gentlemen, gentlemen, I beg you, a little self-control. Kindly stop pestering me, else I shall . . .

(He tries to pick up his sword but realizes that it is no longer in its case. The Selenes break into a rhythmical dance around Cyrano, who tries in vain to break away from their circle.)

DÆMON OF SOCRATES *(off stage, threatening)*

LOUWOO! LOUWOO! LOUWOO!

(Alarmed, the Selenes scatter, letting fall Cyrano's hat and gloves. The Dæmon of Socrates appears. He is wearing a long gown.)

DÆMON OF SOCRATES

Kindly excuse, my lord, these simpletons. They are unaccustomed to visitors. For you have come from the Moon, have you not?

CYRANO

I thank you, sir. *(Thinking about what the other man has said.)* From the Moon? On the contrary, I come from Earth, from a town that is known by the name Paris . . .

DÆMON OF SOCRATES *(interrupting him)*

Ah, Paris . . . I lived in Paris too, once upon a time . . . But I am straying from the point; I am delighted to see you, sir, it has been a long time since I've had the opportunity to converse with a fellow countryman. So long, in fact, that I have got into the habit of referring to the world that is yours as do the inhabitants of this one . . . But you must be exhausted after your long voyage. Very close to here is an inn where you can have something to eat. Allow me to accompany you there.

CYRANO

Gladly, Sir . . . Sir . . . To whom do I have the honour?

DÆMON OF SOCRATES

Several names have been given me in my lifetime: Hélie, Enoch . . . But the one I prefer is without any doubt Daemon of Socrates.

CYRANO

Very well, Mr. Dæmon. My name is Savinien Cyrano de Bergerac.

DÆMON OF SOCRATES

It has been a very long time since I have had a home, but you judged correctly, Monsieur de Bergerac, you are now on what is called, where you come from, the Moon.

ACT 1, SCENE 3

CYRANO
DÆMON OF SOCRATES
INNKEEPER

A salon in the inn, two tables, four chairs, a cooking pot steaming in the hearth. Here, too, everything is white. Cyrano and the Dæmon of Socrates take seats at a table. The innkeeper appears, waves his arm in front of his clients. Cyrano is dumbfounded, but the other man replies by shaking his leg and the innkeeper disappears.

CYRANO
What is the meaning of this pantomime, sir?

DÆMON OF SOCRATES
The language in most common use among these people is expressed by wriggling the limbs, where certain parts of the body signify a complete discourse. Waving one finger, one hand, one ear, one lip, one arm, one cheek, for instance, will make each one in particular an oration, or, if using all one's limbs, a period. Others serve to designate single words, such as a crease on one's brow, the various forms of shuddering of the muscles, the inversions of the hands, the movements of a foot. Accordingly, assuming that you must be very hungry after your journey, I have requested a soup for you. I can moreover smell it drawing near.

CYRANO *(sniffing)*

You are quite right, I smell it too. What a delicious aroma. I truly believe that never in all my life have I been given such a sweet scent to inhale.

DÆMON OF SOCRATES

Very well, indulge yourself.

(Cyrano waits, increasingly impatient. The Dæmon of Socrates stands up.)

CYRANO

I say! Where is that soup, by Jove? Have you made it your challenge to mock me all the day long?

DÆMON OF SOCRATES

I should have thought to warn you: whatever we see here is smoke. The art of cooking is to enclose the exhalations given off by the meats inside large vessels and, having collected several kinds, depending on the appetite of those who are being treated, we discover another and another after that until the entire company is sated. Once the feast is over, we pay in verse.

CYRANO

Ah, now, will you stop mocking me. There is no country, no planet where a verse is common currency, even simply for purchasing some broth.

No, certainly not, but innkeepers are partial to rhymes. And so even when we have feasted here for eight days it would not cost even a sonnet, and I have four with me, along with nine epigrams, two odes, and an eclogue.

(Exeunt.)

Spied yesterday some Esquimaux who have set up their Encampment in proximity to the Terror *and the* Erebus. *They had never seen White Men, and in order to reassure them we had recourse to the Universal Symbol of Good Will, which is a branch of Olive. Once they were reassured, they accepted our Presents and gave us in exchange a revolting piece of Meat which they seemed to believe was an enticing Tidbit. Crozier bit into it. I believe that to please our Hosts he would have eaten Snow should it be necessary.*

Pensive, Sir John rubbed his wrist. Writing tired him. Rereading his words, it struck him that his account did not adequately express the extraordinary nature of the meeting, of the danger avoided, or the spectacular success of his diplomatic venture, all of them matters to which Lady Jane would put the finishing touches should he wish to provide readers a description that was worthy of the events. To give good measure and to direct his wife, he believed it necessary to add:

I have been able Personally to observe that the men are, as has been suspected, perfectly hairless. They are Fierce and made Many Threatening Motions in our direction before at my Suggestion we hoisted the Flag on which appears the Olive Branch and that immediately Pacified them.

To tell the truth, things had not happened exactly in that way; he had not approached closely enough to examine the facial hair of his visitors, but never mind, he was relatively certain that these men had none — and who would contradict him? A significant detail came back to his memory and with his efficient pen he wrote:

Their Smell is most Unpleasant.

FOR THE FIRST TIME since we have been iced in off Beechey Island, we have been visited by Esquimaux. It is obvious that they had never before seen White men or boats or even wood, for they spent long minutes sounding the topsides of the ship as if it were the carcass of a whale.

Their small group comprised three men and two women, one of them repulsive, nearly toothless, which did not stop her from grinning broadly, while the other, younger one could have been pretty had her hair and her skin not been covered with a slick of rancid oil and had her entire being not given off a powerful stench of fish.

They arrived on three sledges pulled by some twenty puny dogs, tongues lolling, next to whom our gallant Neptune looked like a lord. Men and women alike were clad in the skins of animals which they wore in the manner of pelisses, that is to say with the fur turned towards the inside; their mittens and boots were made of skin as well. Spying them, the members of the crew, who for the most part knew of Esquimaux only what they had read in Sir John's narratives — hence very little, if I may to say so — began to let out cries of joy as if they had spied some legendary animal. True, some six months have now passed since we have seen a new face and it is normal that the appearance of a human creature, even if it were an Esquimau, be greeted with explosions of joy. Our hosts showed themselves to be cautious, however, and refused stubbornly, despite our motions and our explanations, to board the ships. Sir John suggested that we hold up on a stick a white flag on which appeared an olive branch, a universal symbol that would signify his peaceful intentions, and whose meaning would be so obvious there would be no question of confusion. I tried to explain to him that these men, having never in their lives seen an olive branch, would not know what to make of this flag, but the thing was prepared in no time at all and held very high. The three men pointed to it and talked among themselves, still not daring to take one step forward. It is difficult to say who among our small group of savages or our own young sailors was the more disconcerted in the presence of the other. A long moment passed that way, in mutual observation. The Esquimaux absolutely did not understand how we had been able to get to where we were. From their gestures and a few words that I recognized, I realized that they were wondering if we had dragged the ships across the ice or if we had arrived from the air.

Sir John then invited me to go ashore with him and attempt to communicate with the savages, but it was a waste of effort. Fascinated by the buttons that adorned our uniforms, they had no use for our words and our pantomimes. Sir John eventually offered a small mirror to the oldest man and the gift was greatly appreciated. Catching sight of his own image in the glass, the man did not rest until he had turned it around and around in every direction, seeking to discover the strange being who was hidden behind or inside it. Still mystified, he finally offered it to the man who was standing at his side so he could plunge his hand into his boot, extracting a piece of dried meat almost violet in colour and offering it in return. Sir John held it out to me without having tasted it, which seemed to disappoint our visitors.

18 March 1846

The Esquimaux have set up their campsite close to the ships, from curiosity perhaps, or self-interest, either because they believe that these huge creatures made of wood will be able to defend them in case of attack, or because they expect new presents from us, having greatly appreciated the caps, buttons, implements, and various baubles that we gave them. The youngest of the women has fixed to a strip of leather, which she wears around her neck, a tin spoon that was given her, and she displays it as if it were the most precious of jewels. They smile continually, even when our men do their best to drive them to distraction. We hear their dogs howling at every hour of the day and night, a song at once disturbing and reassuring, for it shows us that for the first time in months we are no longer alone on the pack ice. Neptune has taken it into his head to answer them and, pointing his muzzle towards the sky and swelling his chops, he produces long ululations to which the choir of other dogs responds in turn.

Yesterday we finally convinced them to come and look around inside the ships. Never have I been given to witness such surprise on a human face. Were they expecting to discover ribs, guts, and organs in the quickwork of the *Terror* and the *Erebus*? There is no way for us to know, for our visitors speak a dialect that is different from, though apparently related to, the one that Blanky, the ice master, and I jabber — very badly, I admit.

There is, however, no need for a translator to understand the lustful gazes that our men direct at the youngest of the young women – whose name is Atsanik – and even, in the case of some, her companion, despite the fact that with her wrinkled face and her mouth bereft of teeth she resembles a prune. Atsanik greets these un-subtle tributes with the good humour that she puts into everything, especially, it seems to me, when they come from the youngest and most graceful seamen. Yesterday I saw her place in Adam's hand a small piece of ivory that she had taken from her coat, then run away laughing like a child. This proximity to women, even if they are Esquimaux, does not augur well in my opinion and I intend to bring it up with Sir John, who should tell them to put up their settlement at a greater distance from us.

LADY JANE HAS NEVER gone out so much. Ever since the departure of her explorer husband people have been lining up at her door and her appointment book is always full. She is the centre of attention at all the parties she attends. The ladies who had greeted her with chilly politeness when she returned from Tasmania, where Sir John had been governor for seven years before being called back abruptly to the home country, no longer dare put on even the most modest tea party without begging her to honour the event with her presence. While she had savoured her revenge during the first months and taken pleasure in accepting their invitations only to withdraw at the last minute, giving as an excuse some vague headache, eventually she found this state of affairs quite normal and refused to stoop so low as to want to antagonize or further humiliate her former enemies. That would be unworthy of her, now that she has become again the wife, not of some obscure official who has been sent home almost in disgrace, but of the hero of the Arctic, the man who had, by Jove, eaten his boots!

And so she accepts most graciously the signs of friendship being lavished on her on all sides, limiting herself — if the reception upon her return from Oceania had been really *too* ill-mannered — to creasing her eyes for a second as if she did not immediately recognize the woman who had spoken to her.

"My dear, how are you? Ah, you do look splendid!" the ladies exclaimed with just a bit of wonder in their voices, as if they were surprised that she had tolerated so well the severity of the Polar climate. Then, thinking perhaps that the hero's wife had at her disposal some means of communication unknown to ordinary mortals that would let her know what progress her illustrious husband had made: "What do you hear?"

Lady Jane would reply impassively that the ships had probably mapped the Lancaster Sound some time ago, or even discovered the entrance to the Passage, that they had no doubt stopped for the winter in some protected bay and would complete their mission once summer came. People walked away murmuring, "What a woman."

When she did not have an invitation to dinner or to tea, or when she herself was not entertaining some member or other of the Royal Society or the Royal Astronomical Society along with his charming wife, a high-ranking officer of the Admiralty accompanied by likewise, or some obscure geographer, cartographer, scientist who was a magnetism and electrical phenomena buff (those most often being old bachelors), Lady Jane would seat herself at the drawing table that had been a gift from Sir John, who had imagined his wife spending delightful hours there painting watercolours, composing acrostics, embroidering, or engaging in some other pleasant feminine pastime. She would spread out in front of her the maps drawn by Scoresby, Ross, and Parry, studying them with the utmost care, noting systematically the differences, inconsistencies, even the most minor variations they displayed. On heavy cream-coloured paper, she drew confidently the coastlines of the land of ice, which were now so familiar to her she could have traced them freehand with her eyes closed. Where the maps diverged she sketched a light, nearly ethereal line to show the various observations and hypotheses of the mariners who had explored these waters since the turn of the century. The strange result was a map of possibilities where in the middle of a sound there rose and did not rise a range of mountains, where a bay was wrapped in similar, larger bays which embraced their miniature twins, like so many Russian dolls, a drunkard's landscape crossed three times by the same river which became one again, briefly, before splitting anew. To find her way in these labyrinthine drawings, Lady Jane had assigned to each of the explorers a colour which she applied more or less strongly depending on how much credit she granted to the depiction of the terrain that he had made. The set of motley lines would have been incomprehensible to anyone but her, and if by chance Sir John had been able to see his wife bent diligently over the paper to which she was applying her colours, he would have thought that she really was devoting herself to painting.

Mr. Bingley and Mr. Darcy were asleep at her feet, their white bellies exposed to the flames crackling in the hearth. Now and then a shudder ran through their long bodies, their paws twitched in uncoordinated movements while they chased some prey in their dreams. Their breathing quickened and at times an ululation rose up, which Lady Jane silenced promptly with a dainty kick from her silken slipper.

Would it have occurred to Miss Jane Griffin to marry John Franklin had not her friend Eleanor Anne Porden shown her, so to speak, the way?

Her first meetings with the famous explorer had barely left an impression, so that she had felt the need, shortly before her marriage, to consult the journal she had kept at the time to strike out some far too nonchalant comments about the man who was destined to become her husband, and to insert elsewhere two or three deliberately vague remarks that could lead one to believe that she had sensed from the outset what an extraordinary individual he was and the no less extraordinary place he would occupy in her life.

In truth, she had been disappointed by the hero of the Arctic. He had returned some months before from the disastrous journey during which four of the men on his expedition had lost their lives in a rather unclear manner, and had just published a somewhat smug account of it when she made his acquaintance. Of medium height, ruddy-faced and corpulent, with a voice that was high and powerful, he was always the first to laugh at his own *bons mots*, which were rare enough. Moreover he was ill-mannered at table and seemed shockingly uninterested in any technical and scientific developments that did not immediately touch on his field of expertise. He never wearied of recounting his adventures – and Jane, hearing him on several occasions describe the same episode to a different audience, could not help noticing that he repeated it in exactly the same words, as if he had written it out, learned it by heart in front of a mirror so as to later narrate it with emphasis – and seemed incapable of paying attention for more than a few minutes to what anyone else had to say. As soon as his interlocutor began to speak he fidgeted, squirming in his seat like a bored child, and soon, unable to take any more, he would interrupt the speaker and launch into a new monologue, holding forth in a stentorian voice. It was impossible not to know how successful the man had been.

One thing was certain, he bore not the slightest resemblance to the intense heroes who filled the novels that delighted Jane, nor to the ethereal characters who were featured in Eleanor's poems. Miss Porden had published, at the age of sixteen, a tremendous tale of some 60,000 lines entitled *The Veils*, which had won the young prodigy immediate recognition and election to the prestigious Institut de France. Eleanor had given a copy of her work to Jane Griffin in the early days of their friendship. It was a strange object, an impassioned ode at once learned and baroque in which romantic exaltation vied with scientific fervour. It was the poem that had driven Jane to seek out the friendship of the younger woman who, while inferior by reason of both station and relations, proved to be, at least, Jane's intellectual equal.

Aged twenty-three when Jane made her acquaintance, Eleanor Anne Porden was a small and dainty person with delicate features and a pale complexion, whose seeming fragility masked a lively mind and a will of iron. Her gentle manner combined exquisite civility with discretion and she expressed herself at all times in a low and musical voice. Jane Griffin had been taken aback to learn, not that the hero of the Arctic was insistently courting the young poetess (which struck Jane as only to be expected), but that the young woman herself, far from doing her best to escape his attentions, accepted them gracefully. If she had been asked to choose a potential husband for her friend, Jane would almost certainly have selected a philosopher with an expressive brow, interested in music and poetry, able to recite the works of the Ancients in Greek; a noble soul, enamoured of the ideal and dedicated to the search for Beauty and Truth.

Sometimes she even wondered if her friend had some secret grounds for marrying; could it be that her family's financial straits were even more severe than Jane suspected? Could it be that she had been *obliged* to consent to this union?

Jane, however, had a change of heart after the marriage — detained out of town, she had been unfortunately unable to attend. (She nonetheless had sent to the couple a lovely silver ewer, along with a letter expressing her regrets and her best wishes for their happiness.) She was told that the ceremony had been surprisingly simple, given the bridegroom's taste for the flamboyant, and that it had been marked only by a slight malaise on the part of the bride, who had quickly recovered. Much admiration had been expressed over the full-length, nearly life-sized self-portrait which Franklin had given to his young wife on the occasion, to replace him when he was absent. It was soon hung in the place of honour in the dining room, where, as Sir John would not go away for several months, it served as a silent twin to its model, nobly surveying the table.

If Jane had feared seeing her friend languish following her marriage, if she had dreaded the young woman's ceding to the influence of her illustrious husband on all matters until she disappeared into his shadow, she was surprised to note that it was he who showed the most visible changes. First of all, he began to appreciate music, although he had never shown signs of the slightest interest in the matter, going so far as to fall asleep as soon as a lady took her seat at the pianoforte. He had also started to purchase pictures and bronzes sensibly, assembling a fine collection within a short period of time. Finally, he, who observed conscientiously the precepts of the Methodist Church – to the point of refusing not only to write a letter on Sunday but even to read a missive addressed to him – agreed, after a brief discussion, that his wife could carry on with her work (which was itself exceptional) and that she might do so on the Lord's Day should that be her wish. Of the young and dashing captains who had married a good many of her friends, very few, Jane knew, would have shown the same understanding, or, perhaps more precisely, the same malleability. What was extraordinary was this: John Franklin was prepared to learn, to change, to improve himself. All that was needed was a firm hand to guide him.

When Eleanor died following a lingering consumption, Jane Griffin had no trouble persuading herself that her friend would have desired more than anything in the world that she, Jane, take her place at the side of her husband and her daughter. Which was done. But it was always in vain that Lady Jane searched the features of Sir John's daughter for the memory of her mother's, with whom she shared nothing but a name. While Eleanor Porden was a lively, sensitive person with keen curiosity and wit, Eleanor Franklin was no more or less than a female version of her father, with his sturdy build, round face, pink complexion, and thick features. Furthermore, she was most often sullen and scowling, and she avoided uttering even a word in the presence of her stepmother unless she was virtually compelled to do so.

The young Eleanor was most often left in the care of a nurse and, when older, entrusted to various relatives with whom she was sent to stay while Jane explored Europe, Africa, or America, or devoted herself entirely to her obligations in London, which left her practically no freedom to saddle herself with a child — *a fortiori* if the child was as lacking in grace as her hapless stepdaughter.

The *VEILS;*

or

THE TRIUMPH OF CONSTANCY

A Poem, in Six Books
by
Miss Porden

Of Earth and Air I sing, of Sea and Fire,
And various wonders that to each belong,
And while to stubborn themes I tune the lyre,
"Fierce wars and faithful loves shall moralize my song."

A YOUNG lady, one of the members of a small society which meets periodically for literary amusement, lost her Veil (by a gust of wind) as she was gathering shells on the coast of Norfolk. This incident gave rise to the following Poem, which was originally written in short cantos, and afterwards extended and modelled into the form in which it is now respectfully submitted to the public. The author, who considers herself a pupil of the Royal Institution, being at that time attending the Lectures given in Albemarle-Street, on Chemistry, Geology, Natural History, and Botany, by Sir Humphry Davy, Mr. Brand, Dr. Roger, Sir James Edward Smith, and other eminent men, she was induced to combine these subjects with her story; and though her knowledge of them was in a great measure orally acquired, and therefore cannot pretend to be extensive or profound, yet, as it was derived from the best teachers, she hopes it will seldom be found incorrect.

The machinery is founded on the Rosicrusian doctrine, which peoples each of the four elements with a peculiar class of spirits, a system introduced into poetry by Pope, and since used by Darwin, in the Botanic Garden; but the author believes that the ideal beings of these two distinguished writers will not be found to differ more from each other, than from those called into action in the ensuing Poem. She has there endeavoured to shew them as representing the different energies of nature, exerted in producing the various changes that take place in the physical world; but the plan of her Poem did not permit her to exhibit them to any considerable extent. On the Rosicrusian mythology, a system of poetical machinery might be constructed of the highest character; but the person who directs its operations should possess the scientific knowledge of Sir Humphry Davy, and the energy and imagination of Lord Byron and Mr. Scott.

In personifying the metals and minerals, and the agency of fire, the author has generally taken her names from the Greek language; but as it was impossible to avoid the nomenclature of modern chemistry, she requests, on the plea of necessity, the indulgence of her readers for what she fears will be felt as a barbarous mixture.

Once, in sweet converse with a knight, I stray'd
Thro' the close windings of a woody glade,
Our hearts by tenderest friendship were allied,
And some few weeks had made me Alfred's bride:
At length with novel charms expands the scene,
The wood retiring left a narrow green;
On either side, with various verdure crowned,
Nor yet by summer's sultry suns embrowned,
Tall hills arise, and thro' the dell below
A crystal river's winding waters flow,
Its banks with flowers adorn'd, and o'er it flung
Its graceful boughs the pendant willow hung.
Charm'd with the scene, beneath the grateful shade,
To cheat the noontide hour, awhile we staid;
The youth was skill'd in vegetable lore,
I ask'd the history of a little flower,
Graceful its form, and bright its lilac hue,
And like the crane's long beak its ripening pistil grew;
The study pleas'd, and from the river's side,
Innumerous flowers our various theme supplied,
The white ranunculus, and iris gay,
The yellow caltha, on the morn of May
That to their homes the cheerful peasants bring,
And strew around, in honour of the spring;
The hyacinth, the violet's purple dye,
And myosotis blue, with golden eye,
Which oft the German youth in graceful knot,
Bears to his love, and sighs 'Forget me not.'

THE HIGHER-RANKING OFFICERS dine on board the *Erebus* as they have done fairly often since the beginning of the Polar night. The conversation of course revolves around the Esquimaux based nearby. Little and Gore are as thrilled as children at their arrival. One would swear that they had discovered some mythical creature – a white whale, a unicorn – that they knew only from books, and that this meeting has taken them into legend. Sir John has seen others, of course, he who has travelled for weeks in the company of savages, as has Crozier, the only one who understands bits of their strange and guttural language.

In spite of the cold and the darkness, the mood is nearly festive. Admittedly there has been no fresh meat for a long time, but the men continue to feast on salted seabirds of which the violet flesh, seasoned with cinnamon and clove, is somewhat reminiscent of deer; then there are the tasty stews that the cook prepares for the officers from dried meats and some of Mr. Goldner's canned goods. In some of the cans bits of bone and rind have been found; one galley boy even swears that he discovered an eye, which Neptune swallowed before he could show it to anyone, but the contents of these tins of dubious quality will feed the seamen, the choicest morsels of course being reserved for the Captain's table.

As candles are precious, the holders on the walls stay dark and only a single three-branched candelabrum in the centre of the table is lit, its light casting shifting shadows onto the walls.

DesVoeux, who has had the leisure to observe the Esquimaux

over the past days, is surprised that such primitive creatures have been able to survive in an environment like the Arctic. There commences then, for the hundredth time, a discussion about the flaws and the fine qualities of savage peoples which, started shortly after they embarked, is now taken up again and again, developed and expounded upon, each man remaining fiercely attached to positions that are relinquished when weariness sets in, only to be picked up afresh, the way that ladies will go back to a piece of embroidery or knitting. Gore suggests that an attempt be made to establish relations with one or two groups – preferably made up only of men or, in a pinch, with old women who are not very enticing – who would no doubt be useful to the ships' crews. DesVoeux resists:

"How can one trust savages who live like animals?"

"It is indeed true that, like animals," begins Sir John learnedly, in a timid attempt to please both sides, "they have an innate talent for hunting. They know how to track prey for days and how to survive in inhuman conditions. But it is true as well that they know neither order nor beauty and they respect no God other than their animal spirits."

"Among several peoples," Crozier intervenes, "legends tell that the Earth was inhabited first by animals and that man did not come until afterwards."

"The Bible, for example!" retorts Fitzjames, whose remark is greeted with thunderous laughter.

Sir John does not join in the hilarity; there are some things that do not lend themselves to laughter. He regrets, however, that he has no pen with which to note the principal arguments exchanged during this conversation, which promises to be particularly lofty and which, he is certain, will delight his wife, with her keen interest in rhetoric.

"Quite right," agrees Gore once calm is restored. "And therein lies the fundamental difference: while God made us masters of all that exists upon this Earth, their false divinities force them to submit to whatever they find around them. For that reason they will never know progress and will continue forever to pace the icefield clad in the skins of beasts, whereas we have conquered the globe."

Crozier adds, "They may be primitive but they take marvellous advantage of the meagre resources offered by this environment: they dress in the skins of animals whose flesh they eat, they use the tallow and the fat of those animals to provide light, their bones for making needles and various small tools. They even build their houses from what they try to escape, for they use snow to protect themselves from the cold."

Farlone is unconvinced.

"I grant you, of course, that they are capable of building an igloo from snow and ice and of hiding away there like the bear in its den. But there is nothing remarkable about that. Show me a city of snow or a palace of ice, and I will acknowledge that these savages may be seen as genuine men. They have no notion of society, which is the very mark of civilization, since they live and move about in groups of five or six, in dozens if need be, accompanied by five times as many dogs . . ."

"Moreover," notes Hornby, "they do not hesitate to eat them in the event that they run out of food."

Crozier seems dubious. Someone bends over his shoulder to take his empty plate while someone else uncorks a new bottle of wine.

Henceforth, Sir John follows the conversation more distractedly. He feels that his liver is rather congested.

"I, too," replies Fitzjames, "have heard stories recounting that dogs had been sacrificed by hunters who were short of meat and unable to kill a seal – and perhaps it did happen, but I find it difficult to believe that it is standard practice. First of all, the Esquimaux need their animals too much to dispose of any in that manner; and then they are very close to their dogs. The dogs are their true companions."

"Ah yes, precisely!" DesVoeux breaks in, clicking his tongue. "That is one more piece of evidence, should one be needed, that those individuals are closer to wild animals than they are to civilized men: birds of a feather do flock together, after all, and one must be something of a dog oneself to share the life of four-footed animals in that way."

Struck with nostalgia, Sir John sees again in memory Mr. Darcy and Mr. Bingley, asleep at the foot of Lady Jane's bed. It seems to him, on the contrary, that these small creatures have been significantly humanized by contact with his wife. Be that as it may, she would no doubt not appreciate this last interruption. He will omit it from his presentation.

Crozier, though, does not intend to let it go.

"That phenomenal ability to adapt to extraordinarily inhospitable nature, to make use of the least of its resources, living in harmony with it all the while, testifies to a form of, while not, strictly speaking, intelligence, at the very least common sense and ingenuity."

He breaks off, out of breath. A brief silence settles in

around the table; no one had expected him to be so eloquent. Sir John gestures to ask for more port wine. Then DesVoeux speaks up again, his tone slightly mocking.

"Really?" he asks. "Adaptability – that is to say plasticity, in a word, flexibility – is the criterion whereby we should judge the degree of inventiveness of a people? If that be so I know of no creatures more highly evolved than our friends the fish, who are so wonderfully well equipped for living underwater, whereas we can survive for no more than a few minutes!"

Again, thunderous laughter greets this outburst and each then goes him one better:

"Or bears, whose stocks of grease let them survive the winter without eating!"

"Or the oyster, whose shell is a genuine suit of armour for the flabby animal it encloses . . ."

"Or the chameleon, who assumes at will the colours of the foliage on the tree where he is perching!"

"No," DesVoeux starts up again, after savouring his triumph and slamming his empty sherry glass onto the table, "the ability to adapt to one's environment, while far from being a sign of a people's degree of advancement, is on the contrary the sign of its primitivism. Civilization consists not of submitting to the whims of Nature, on that you will agree with me, but forcing it to bend to our needs, to overpower it and constrain it."

He looks Crozier straight in the eye, who suddenly thinks of Sophia with painful acuteness. He clenches his fists and tries to respond but the other man has not finished:

"That is how we can build ships that are able to cut through the ice rather than merely travel across it, drawn by dogs. That is how we can write books that give an account of our discoveries and provide information for those who will come after us."

DesVoeux turns his gaze towards Sir John, who puffs himself up, before dealing out the coup de grâce: "That is how cities and empires are built. That is how we triumph over chaos and ensure the rule of law!"

Half rising, DesVoeux makes a slight bow, seeming to mock himself for having given in to such ardent declarations, but, meeting his gaze as he is getting to his feet, Crozier sees only chilly satisfaction.

A smiling Sir John congratulates himself once again on having among his crew such perceptive men.

Crozier is pensive. He is not quick at repartee like DesVoeux, whose sparkling wit he admires. He needs to nurture his opinions at length before he can put them into words and defend them. He cannot deny that having a strict ability to adapt to one's environment could not be taken for proof of intelligence, but he is still convinced that there is a lesson to be learned from this form of fundamental humility.

Excusing himself, he withdraws while another bottle of port is being uncorked. Below decks, the hammocks have been hung up for the night and most of the men are already asleep. A few are talking in low voices; others are snoring or moaning in their sleep, where a fearsome beast or a delectable damsel has come to visit them. On the ground can be seen the fleeting shadows of rats that come out only at night. From the galley come the usual sounds and smells. The next day's bread is being prepared.

Crozier's cabin, like those of all the officers, is minute. A narrow bunk stands against the back wall, on top of a large drawer, the only storage space, where clothing and linen are piled up, along with a Bible that had belonged to his father and his grandfather before him and in which he keeps a daguerreotype of Sophia Cracroft that he has held in his hands so often that the edges are worn thin and faded; rabbit skin mittens that his sister, full of goodwill, had made for him and that he refuses to get rid of though he is unable to slip his hands inside them; and the first compass given him by William Parry, the warped needle of which points forever towards the west.

On a tiny shelf next to the bed sit a razor, shaving brush, pomade, soap, and a small mirror. A writing desk stands against the wall in such a way as to take up as little space as possible. On the wall is an engraving of the Irish countryside, a place called Oughterard where he has never gone but where he dreams of settling down and enjoying an unexciting old age, imagining himself pruning his roses and hunting partridge in the company of his dogs while Sophia embroiders in the garden.

He undresses, teeth chattering. The heat is kept as low as possible. The temperature was bearable in the big room where the men sleep packed together, but the cabins are ice-cold – the reason why Mayfair, on board the *Erebus,* is in the habit of bringing to his cabin a galley boy who, he says, acts as a hot water bottle.

Crozier is well aware that these things happen commonly on boats, even between men who are not inclined that way. Nevertheless, on his ship, each man sleeps in his bunk or in his hammock, and those who violate the rule must go without their ration of toddy for a week.

Still shivering, he slips between the sheets which have not been laundered for weeks, hot water being measured. He pulls over himself a rough wool blanket made by the Hudson's Bay Company and opens his Bible to take out the picture of Sophia. Holding it before his eyes he runs his right hand over his belly, imagining that the fingers closing around his sex are hers. His muffled moans join the sighs that rise from a hundred bodies given over to the Polar night.

AT THE BEGINNING of April, Sophia was invited, as she was each year, to spend a week at Halsway Manor in Sussex by her cousin, who was bored to death during the rest of the year with a husband enamoured of hunting and horses but with no interest in society, by which he meant any contact with other human beings that was not strictly necessary. On the birthday of his young wife, however, he invited her two childhood friends to the manor and allowed the ladies to indulge in as many teas, balls, and other delights as they wished.

Sophia and Amelia set out together from London, each accompanied by a trunk in which she had found room for a good part of her wardrobe, for spring is a treacherous season; there can be a hard frost one morning and radiant sun the next. It was best therefore to be prepared for all eventualities. Sophia, having developed over the years habits she found it hard to shed, took along her pillows filled with gosling down (the only kind that was agreeable to the delicate nape of her neck), a black velvet eye mask which she slipped on for sleeping (unable to tolerate the light that seeped in through her bedroom curtains at dawn), and a tin of Darjeeling tea, which she offered as a gift for her hostess but that she had taken care to bring mainly because she refused to ingest the insipid mixture that the latter offered at breakfast time.

Upon their arrival the guests were offered a light meal and had the leisure to chat until bedtime. Starting the next morning, however, the round of activities would begin and would go on for seven days, after which the ladies would depart.

Around eight o'clock some discreet knocks are struck at each young woman's door, accompanied by murmured enquiries as to whether Madame wants anything. If necessary, the knocking will be repeated a little more vigorously until an intelligible response comes from the room. Basins of hot water are brought so the ladies can perform their ablutions; the chambermaids dexterously handle crinolines, petticoats, corsets, and other essential accessories and soon the young women are ready to go down to breakfast.

Shortly afterwards come stockists, who make the most of this week when there are guests at the manor to display their softest silks, their most irresistible jewels, their finest gloves. Sophia generally allows herself to be tempted by some trinket that she will forget about once she is back in London, while Elizabeth takes advantage of the manna to stock up on collars, lace, and hats for the coming year. The ladies then go out to stroll in the gardens surrounding the manor where they may see does with large astonished eyes, pheasants, partridges – all at risk of ending up on the dinner table. They walk briskly to whet their appetites, for lunch will be copious.

They sit at table on the stroke of one o'clock for the main meal of the day, which consists most often of a fish course followed by one of the animals encountered earlier, roasted, accompanied by vegetables from the garden; the ladies then withdraw to freshen up and take a nap, a brief one, for the rest of the day is organized to a fare-thee-well.

The carioles are brought up in the middle of the afternoon and they set off to visit one of the many nearby squires, delighted to entertain such young and joyful company, or they will admire some modest attraction in a neighbouring village. The weather is particularly mild for the season and the young women delight in these excursions when they may discover in the corner of a square a fountain, a stained-glass church window, a tiny museum devoted to a nearly first-rate painter, illustrious son and pride of the village, a china factory, or the ruins of a medieval dungeon. From the gently rounded flanks of the hills they gaze at the panorama that is offered to the strollers: in the valley drowned in the golden light of the approaching spring the budding trees wear haloes of a very pale green mist; the grey and russet houses are nestled close together; plumes of smoke rise up from their chimneys in swirls, like bundles of fur.

They come back to the manor at dusk. Tea awaits madam and her friends, who, ravenous from the pure country air, devour sandwiches and biscuits, then each goes up to her room to dress for evening, since the guests will arrive shortly, unless a neighbouring family is having a ball or a soirée.

Sophia asks again for hot water which the servants bring up, grumbling (Why does that woman think she's so dirty that she feels the need to soak her body morning and night? His Lordship bathes only once a month and is none the worse for it), then she does her hair herself. The festivities get underway around eight o'clock and will continue until well past midnight, the hour when Elizabeth's husband, who likes to rise with the sun, will go to bed, after dozing in an armchair all evening.

The ladies meet again to share a light meal before they go to bed. As they savour terrines, pâtés, mousses, cheeses, and cold meats, accompanied by wines from Burgundy, they review the most striking events of the evening. The fires in the bedrooms are stirred up, hot water bottles are brought, and soon the three friends slip under their eiderdowns and fall into a deep sleep from which they will be drawn in the morning by some discreet knocks on the door.

And thus unfolds life at Halsway Manor during this spring of the year 1846.

5 April 1846

THIS MORNING A THIRD grave was added to the two crosses whose bare arms stand out against the white sky. William Braine, aged thirty-three, was found lifeless in his bunk yesterday morning. I am told that all last week he suffered from diarrhea and cramps, vomiting yellowish bile, as did four other mariners whose condition seems less disturbing but whom Peddie has nonetheless placed under observation in the infirmary.

Once again the crews gathered in silence on the rocky soil of Beechey Island to leave behind one of their own. I cannot help imagining that this sterile island will not be satisfied until it has swallowed the bodies of the 126 men who are walking upon it today. More than ever I am eager to leave this cursèd land and go to sea again. In a few weeks the ice that clasps the *Erebus* and the *Terror* will perhaps have relaxed its grip and we shall be able to leave and, God willing, enter the passage that no one is even certain exists, but in the reality of which I must now believe if I am not to succumb to despair, and return at last to England. As I write these words I realize that even that desire is not entirely pure for I well know that upon our return I shall be obliged to see the joy and admiration in Sophia's eyes at the sight of Fitzjames, returned safe and sound. Yet I do not hate him now and have never hated him; I wish him no harm; rather, I value his company: his mood is cheerful and he is a fine companion. Chance has made him handsome while it has made me what I am.

AFTER BECOMING ACQUAINTED with all the books in the *Terror*'s library, after solving the problems set forth in the manuals of physics and mathematics, after considering the paradoxes submitted by treatises in philosophy, after reading and rereading the *Sonnets* of Shakespeare until he could recite most of them by heart, Adam set out to devote himself to what had fascinated him beyond anything else ever since he had discovered the fundamental principles in several theoretical studies. It seemed to him that all the rest (mathematical formulæ, philosophical allegories, geographical observations, and even poetry) were but imperfect illustrations of this one phenomenon: magnetism. He had spotted the instruments that Crozier and the officers used in taking various readings and he had many times listened to them discuss the problems and the pitfalls of the task, which was long and complex, and now he had managed to develop a fairly accurate idea of how it was done.

Beginning for the tenth time the introduction to the most ordinary method of declination, he spoke the words in a hushed voice without really reading them, almost as if it were a dictation:

The value of the terrestrial field is usually determined by the declination and the inclination, which give the directions, and by the value of one component. It would also be sufficient to know the declination and two of the components.

In order to have the declination, the geographical meridian must first be determined, and then the azimuth in which the magnetic axis of a magnet sets movable about a vertical axis. This latter observation usually presents some difficulties, since the magnetic axis of a magnet is not generally parallel to its axis of figure; the error is corrected by turning the magnet upside down, observing in each position the direction of a line of sight; the mean of the two azimuths is the line which passes through the magnetic axis.

The line of sight is formed either by the ends of a needle, cut in the shape of an acute lozenge, or by two cross wires at the ends of a bar, as in Gambey's compass; or by two lines traced on the terminal faces of the magnet, and which are viewed with the microscope. We may also use hollow bars, converted into collimators by an object-glass let into one end, and a divided scale or a cross wire at the other.

Suppose, for instance, that we merely know the latitude of the place. Let OP be the earth's axis, OA the vertical, OE the direction of the star at the moment of observation, l the latitude of the place or the height of the pole, h the height EQ of the star.

In the spherical triangle APE, the PA is equal to 90° − l, the side AE to 90° − h, the side EP is at the polar distance Δ of the star, or the complement of its declination. The angle h is given by the vertical circle, and the corresponding reading of the verniers is made on the horizontal circle.

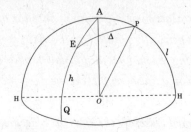

Putting

$$h + l + \Delta = 2S,$$

the angles A and P will be given by the formulæ

$$\cos \frac{A}{2} = \sqrt{\frac{\sin S \cos (S - \Delta)}{\cos l \cos h}}$$

$$\sin \frac{P}{2} = \sqrt{\frac{\sin S \cos (S - h)}{\cos l \sin \Delta}}$$

He took pleasure in slowly dissecting these formulæ, deciphering the instructions with fascination, as if they would enable him to reach the philosopher's stone, with the absolute certainty that they were leading to some fundamental revelation about the secret life that hummed in the heart of the Earth.

These equations contained another kind of poetry that, Adam was certain, was not a stranger to the art practised by Shakespeare, who would no doubt have known better than he did the mysteries of a true bearing.

22 May 1846

IMMACULATE UPON OUR ARRIVAL, the ice around the ships now
resembles in places a wasteland of the sort one finds in poor
neighbourhoods; the pack ice that surrounds us is strewn with
all kinds of trash: empty tins, bits of oakum and rope now
unusable, gloves mismatched or left to dry in the sun and forgotten – not to mention the contents of hundreds of chamber
pots (even though we had ordered that they be emptied in a
single spot some hundreds of feet from the ships), which here
and there form small mounds of filth that fortunately are frozen.
When I raised the question with Sir John this afternoon, suggesting that we put together a work crew for the purpose of
cleaning up this waste, he gave me a look of surprise as if he
had just noticed its existence and asked me how I intended to
dispose of it – indeed, he was quite right to do so and I did not
press him further. But the sight of it spreading over the icefield
turns my stomach; I have the impression at times that the contents of the ship's entrails are being poured onto the snow like
black bile thrown up by a sick man's stomach.

1 June 1846

Nearly every week, weather permitting, one or two small
groups are dispatched with the mission of taking magnetic
readings for a given territory. The instruments used are

complex and fragile and one must have the patience of Job in order to stay motionless, often for hours, on the pack ice; to handle with tremendous care compass, needle, roulettes that are hard for numb fingers to pick up. As this task also requires rather advanced mathematical skills, some twenty men at most are capable of performing it successfully. I try to organize them into teams, the composition of which varies from one time to the next, and not to favour anyone, but I cannot ignore the fact that those fortunate mortals who are able to escape for a few days the stale atmosphere of the ships are the envy of the others. For my part, I have gone out only three times on similar expeditions that lasted for two or three days, and each time I came back filled with wonder at how vast are the spaces that we claim to control.

The undertaking appears to be at once necessary and absurd. Will it be possible one day to consult an atlas of the Earth's magnetic fields as easily as, today, a map showing coasts, tides, currents, and mountains? Will the underground forces whose functions we are only beginning to understand help us to better orient ourselves on this Earth, or do they only form a new labyrinth in which to lose one's way?

The maps that we are drawing have as their central point the place where the *Terror* and the *Erebus* are iced in, from which are added, in concentric circles, new observations as they are recorded. We must therefore enter ever more profoundly into the savage depths of the Arctic so as to complete our readings. The last time, we witnessed a most peculiar phenomenon, which I recognized only because I had read the account in Ross's book (and I have to admit, to my brief shame, that I remember thinking that the description of it was so spectacular it could only be an exaggeration). In the middle of the plain covered with bluish snow were vast red expanses, or, more precisely, they were a pink that was nearly fuchsia, reminiscent of watermelons. Like Ross, I can attest that we have not witnessed any pink snowfall since we have been here, that is to say for nearly a year, and so that strange hue must come from the ground itself, affected by some chemical reaction, a remarkable substance or an animal or vegetable compound. Whatever it is, the result is most astonishing, and one would swear that watermelon flesh has been mashed to a rose-coloured pulp mixed with snow where in certain spots it traces darker veins of the sort one may see in marble, then in a subtle gradation it blurs, forming a rosaceous monochrome against a white ground.

Peddie is certain that this hue is due to the presence of microscopic plants or pollens that colour the snow, as does the pistil of a crocus plunged into a liquid which straightaway turns a warm gold. As for me, I do not know much save that this peculiar phenomenon, which is a source of concern to a number of individuals (some seamen talk about "the Earth's blood," crossing themselves, others make reference to hypothetical places of sacrifice of the Esquimaux, or mysterious places where herds are slaughtered, leaving an imprint on the snow), inspires no fear in me. It seems thoroughly at home here among the wonders that the Arctic conceals. This morning we also noticed a group of narwhals – veritable unicorns of the sea – which are no less surprising than the red snow. The men tried to kill one but were able only to inflict a rather nasty wound and it got away, leaving behind a red trail in the water.

Pity, for we are desperately short of fresh meat. Moreover, the Esquimaux hold in high esteem the horn of this animal, from which they make a multitude of tools, and we would doubtless have been able to trade that good-sized horn for seal meat or fish. That will be for another time: life seems to be reborn in the water as on Earth. Polar nature, dead for more than six months, drowned in the shadows, experiences in summer a brief yet spectacular rebirth. Flocks of birds fill the sky. On the land freshly rid of snow appears a miniature flora as diverse as that which composes our stately forests; it is simply, one might say, that everything in it has been reduced, the better to resist inclement wind and cold. As soon as the ice has loosened its embrace of the hulls of the *Erebus* and *Terror,* we shall be able to set off again and complete the passage started last year.

Did Franklin receive orders about what name to give the mystic way? Oddly enough, I have never asked myself. If it is so, he has said nothing about it to me. I would be surprised if Barrow, who has a well-earned reputation for seeing to the smallest detail and attending to every eventuality, would have left unresolved so important a matter. I am certain he would have liked the Northwest Passage, the discovery of the century, which has perhaps no equal in history but the discovery of America, to bear his name, but I doubt that pride would have blinded him to such a point that he would have seriously considered this possibility. Rather, he would have chosen to name it in honour of the young Queen Victoria, with whom it is said that he is infatuated. True, she is quite pretty, but very frail and inexperienced for holding firmly on to the reins of so powerful a nation.

Today the sky is a deep, sharp blue unknown to the skies of England or Ireland, its hard brilliance reminiscent of the lakes in which the minerals imprisoned in glaciers or earth for millennia have dissolved. The sea that surrounds us, still covered with ice, has lost none of its whiteness, so that you could believe that a mischievous or absent-minded giant has turned the globe upside down to pour into the vault of heaven the blue waters of the sea and cast into the waters the white of the clouds. Oh, how I long to set sail again and to return to the open sea, my true homeland.

12 July 1846

It is hard to hold my pen and even more to trace these words with fingers still numb after I have spent these past days buried under the snow and then exposed to the elements, but I want to tell what happened and I must force myself to write.

We had reckoned on this expedition for a fortnight, waiting for the most auspicious climatic conditions for successful magnetic readings, taking with us rations enough to feed the five men who made up the team that I had myself put together for more than a week. When I told Adam that he would be coming with us, he could not stand still for joy. These past weeks he had been studying day and night the operation of Brunner's compass and Gambey's and the formulæ needed for calculating the declination; I had no doubts as to his technical skill.

Peddie had also insisted on coming with us, pointing out that he had never yet been able to get away from the vessels in summer and that he knew practically nothing about the flora and fauna in that season. When I explained to him a little harshly that we had better things to do than run around the fields picking flowers for his herbarium, he replied calmly that one never knew in advance what plant might be liable to save our lives, and that it would be to our advantage to learn about all of those around us while there was still time. I do not know if he was alluding to the too-brief Arctic summer which soon would be replaced by winter, or to some other certainty that was equally unavoidable but more widespread. Never mind, he was right, and I resolved to bring him along.

I must stop writing to blow on my stiff red fingers although it is useless. It feels as though the cold that pierces me to the bone will never really go away. I shall have to warm my hands for a few moments on the steaming cup of tea that has just been placed in front of me before I can go on.

We set out then in the early hours, before the first rays of dawn, and headed north, with the intention of exploring the interior of Beechey Island, which we have not yet had the opportunity to survey. Neptune pranced about at our sides and I was unable to send him back to the ship. At my command he would sit for a few seconds, looking woeful, then come running back to us, frenetically wagging his tail. And so our team was enriched by a dog. The ground, frozen when we left, warmed up after noon and the icy plains gave way to soft bogs where we sank in to the ankles. We took a first series of readings during the afternoon, then we established our camp for the night.

The next three days passed without incident. The men were

delighted to get away from the confined quarters where they had spent the winter crammed together, and I must confess that I, too, was pleased to be surrounded by vast expanses, alone with them under a huge sky shot through now and then by a flight of wild birds. Our small crew worked quickly and well, avoiding pointless chatter. Everyone knew what had to be done and did it without my having to remind anyone of the task that had devolved upon him. Even Peddie surprised me by the relevance and the aptness of his observations, and I congratulated myself for having agreed that he be part of the expedition. The temperature was relatively mild and the gusts of wind were mitigated by the rays of spring sunlight that were gaining in strength day by day.

On the morning of the fourth day, when we had to go back, we had ventured farther from the *Terror* and the *Erebus* than I had originally expected, but I had decided to take advantage of such a fine opportunity to cover as much ground as possible. As dawn was fading the sound of the wind wakened me and I stepped out of the tent to discover a world that was uniformly white. The snow had covered everything and the landscape had lost its fine edge so that one could now make out only slight undulations; it was impossible to tell whether they corresponded to genuine inclinations of the ground or if they were dunes of snow formed by the wind. We ate our porridge of oats and drank our tea in the partial shelter of our tents where swept the gusts of wind laden with thousands of flakes as hard as ice. Then we struck camp and started back. We had to stop after a few hours, however; we could not see two feet in front of us, and the snow that covered everything was liable to conceal deep crevasses as well. We pitched our tents again but no sooner had we put up the second than the first took flight in the wind that lifted it from the ground and carried it off like a great bird with clumsy wings. So all five of us piled into the only shelter that was left us. I inspected what remained of our rations, which would not last much longer. Along with a half-pound of tea and about a pound of chocolate, there were a dozen rations of biscuits and four two-pound tins of food. Calculating that it had taken us three days at a good clip to reach the place where we were, we had provisions enough to wait one more day, two at most, before setting off again.

The day was spent listening to the howling wind which, far from dropping, seemed to be more and more violent. Our tent was more than half buried by the snow that was falling without interruption, and when I could not keep still any longer and tried to go out and reconnoitre the surroundings, I sank in up to my knees and could move only with difficulty, each step requiring a substantial effort. As the tent was too small for five men to lie down in it side by side, the others took turns sleeping while I spent the night sitting and thinking about what we should do. Admittedly we were in no immediate danger, but we were faced with a three-day walk and very little to eat (I cursed the nonchalance that had made me insist that we take only light baggage), and who could say how long this blizzard would last? I resolved then that we would start walking again the next morning, whatever the weather.

It was a grave error. The snow was falling less heavily but the temperature had dropped significantly, and after less than an hour's walk, our heavy wool trousers, soaked in sweat and then frozen by the intense cold, had been transformed into stiff, rough armour that hampered our movements, already rendered difficult by the accumulation of snow. We sank up to our thighs with each step, and in order to advance we had to perform a strange dance – free one leg from the sheath of snow that it had dug, make it trace an arc, before projecting it forward in one movement. It was as if we were all afflicted with two wooden legs.

There was no more trace of the birds seen over the preceding days or of any other living creature. The cold was biting and soon I could no longer feel the tips of my fingers. The men's faces were daubed with white blotches and red marks, but nonetheless it seemed to me advisable to keep going at all costs. It was practically impossible to know with certainty what distance we had covered – it was no doubt minimal – but at least we were walking in the right direction, which provided me with the illusion, in any case, that we were improving our lot.

We went on like that for some hours, without stopping, until I heard a cry behind me. Turning around, I spied only three silhouettes. Jeremy Welling was sunk to his chest in a slushy mess of water, snow, and ice. Adam had flung himself nimbly onto his stomach and started crawling to the other man, who was trying desperately to grip the edge of the hole but in doing so succeeded only in enlarging it, thereby jeopardizing his rescue. I managed to persuade him to jettison the bag he was carrying on his back, which disappeared at once beneath the surface of the water, and to stop moving.

Nearly suspended above the hole, Adam, held by Tinker,

who had firmly caught hold of his legs, finally came close enough to Jeremy that the latter was able to grasp his hand and slowly emerge. His lips were blue and his entire body was shivering. There was no question of going on. We pitched the tent not far from there, in a safe place, and succeeded in making a fire on which I brewed sweetened tea. We took off Jeremy's soaking-wet clothes, which had frozen on him as soon as he emerged from the water. I realized at that moment that the bag he was carrying and which I had urged him to get rid of contained a good half of our rations.

We had brought no change of clothes and those that we had on our backs were hardly less sodden than his. We wrapped him in a woollen blanket and rubbed him down as best we could.

The shudders that ran through his body died down after a few hours but he had sunk into delirium and was murmuring incoherently, feebly beating the air with his arms as if to drive away a swarm of flies that only he could hear. Peddie urged us to continue rubbing him down in order to speed up the circulation of his blood, which doubtless was no longer irrigating the brain as it should, and we took turns at his side.

A few hours later, through the wind which was again howling and snapping the tent canvas, I thought I heard barking. I went out and discovered three sledges, each one pulled by a dozen dogs, on which were perched six Esquimaux. I was happy to recognize Atsanik, Kavik, Ugjuk, and Kapilruq, who had visited us last winter and whom we had then seen as boisterous, rather entertaining children. It seemed to me that we had been saved.

They urged us to climb onto their sledges but I refused to

leave behind our tent, and we struck it quickly in order to carry it away with us. In the meantime they hitched Neptune to one of the sledges, beside their skinny, high-strung dogs, but instead of pulling with them, he shook himself, arched his back, and finally dropped to the ground, then was dragged across the snow by his fellow creatures, who did not slow down for something so minor. Ashamed, I asked, using signs, if we could stop long enough to free him. Our saviours seemed to think that I was getting ready to abandon him on the pack ice but I was able to make them understand that, actually, I wanted to put him on the sleigh with us. The man who was driving us roared with laughter, but the others seemed rather incensed. Nonetheless, Neptune was set down next to me and he spent the rest of the journey, which was brief, seated comfortably. We stopped less than an hour later in a sort of basin protected from the wind. There, while the women were wrapping Jeremy in furs and fixing for him a brew of dried herbs, the men began to construct two igloos that would serve us as shelters for the night.

Little by little some sensitivity comes back, painfully, to my fingertips, and I am so tired that I can no longer see what I am writing. I must stop here for the night and continue tomorrow when I am rested.

I spent the night between sleep and wakefulness, visited in my dreams by Sophia and by those Esquimaux who, I am convinced, saved our lives. Curled up on a blanket at the foot of my bunk where normally he does not sleep, Neptune has not got to his feet for fifteen hours. He is snoring. As for me, I am stiff with aches and pains, still unable to swallow anything save hot tea but ready to resume my narrative.

I had already observed these rudimentary structures which the Esquimaux build but I had never taken part in their construction: I must confess that while their igloos appear to be primitively or even crudely simple, they nonetheless evince a form of genius. While the women were watching over Jeremy, Kavik showed us how to cut blocks of snow of equal size and secure them carefully in such a way as to create a perfect dome, from which the top is then removed, creating a chimney through which smoke may escape. It is nearly miraculous: the whole structure, from which the keystone, a crucial and essential component of any construction, has been removed, does not collapse and loses none of its solidity. Perhaps with the hope of impressing us, Kapilruq also showed us how to make a most respectable window using a translucent piece of ice.

On the inside, these houses are strangely cozy. The atmosphere is muffled, bluish, similar to that which must exist underwater. An even more peculiar marvel, they provide very effective protection from the cold, and not only do they offer a bastion against the wind, they also preserve the warmth in such a way that at all times the temperature is around 40 degrees Fahrenheit. The Esquimaux light fires there with no fear of melting the walls or the roof.

Regardless of DesVoeux's scoffing I cannot help but be filled with admiration when I think that these men do not know cities, that they roam endlessly, constructing here and there short-lived houses of snow in a barren landscape where they are able to survive, lacking everything, at the mercy of the elements and of inhospitable nature, in this land abandoned by God.

Once the igloos had been built, we took refuge therein to spend the night. I occupied the larger of the two, along with Jeremy, who, perhaps thanks to the concoction administered to him by the women, was no longer delirious and appeared to be sleeping quietly; with Peddie, who continued to keep watch over him; with the youngest of the women; and with Ugjuk, who I believed was her husband.

While outside the dogs were barking and howling at the moon, Ugjuk and Atsanik invited us to share their meagre sustenance: dried meat of caribou, tough as leather, which had to be sucked for a long time before one could begin to masticate it – in spite of myself I had a thought just then for Sir John, and for the first time the words "the man who ate his boots" seemed to me not so much ridiculous as desperate – and a gruel based on seal fat, a preparation that was heavy and indigestible but hot, and so more than welcome. After the meal, our hosts conversed rapidly in their language, then Ugjuk wrapped himself in the skins that had been spread on the ground and went to sleep. Jeremy had opened his eyes and taken a few mouthfuls of gruel before being swallowed up again in sleep, soon imitated by Peddie who was lying beside him.

Lying on my back I gazed at the fire glinting off the walls of snow, realizing that for the first time in three days I was not suffering from the cold, when I heard the rustling of furs. Atsanik had half risen, the lowness of the igloo making it impossible to stand, and came and lay down beside me. Surprised, I glanced, concerned, at Ugjuk nearby, a glance to which she responded with a smile. She then began to undress in silence, removing the skins in which she was clad as naturally and as gracefully as a lady taking off her gloves and hat when she comes home.

Dumbfounded, I dared not make a move, and she stayed for a long moment looking at me, smiling, her breasts round like oranges (which she has no doubt never seen), her long black oily hair falling over her shoulder, her dark eyes staring at me without blinking. And then . . . My pen dares not trace the words that would be necessary for recounting what then took place, but for several minutes I forgot where I was — and that Jeremy had nearly died, that the lives of five men and another hundred were in my hands, that our rations and supply of coal were getting low, that the ice was not disappearing, that Sophia will never love me even if I return as a hero. And I slept a dreamless sleep for the first time in months.

It took three days to get back to the ships. During the day, Atsanik paid no particular attention to me, but she came back and lay at my side in the night, contenting herself with curling up against me like a small animal, her nose buried in my neck.

Fitzjames was preparing to dispatch a rescue expedition when we finally returned to the *Terror* and the *Erebus*. The Esquimaux were generously rewarded with two rifles, a lieutenant's tunic with gold buttons, five tin cups, an axe, sugar, and rum, after they had refused, gesturing broadly, the tinned goods that we offered them. They saved our lives, and I do not know if I will ever see them again.

"MMF."

It was not exactly a sigh, and it most certainly was not an exclamation of surprise; barely a slight discharge of air, actually, that marked a restrained amazement.

Sophia did not look up from the newspaper she held, folded, in front of her, where she was reading a laudatory review of a play she had seen the week before, which had struck her as rather mediocre. As she did every morning, she took her breakfast with her aunt in the room arranged for that purpose at the back of the house on Bedford Street. As these ladies were not the sort who believed that a healthy appetite showed a lack of refinement or was the sign of an unrefined soul, the table set for two was laden copiously with scones, toasted bread, ham, sautéed kidneys, scrambled eggs, mushrooms, a terrine of pheasant, and some leftover eel pâté – a still life that was lit up by the first rays of sunlight shining through the vast windows on all sides of the small dining room that was furnished simply and lined with orange trees in pots that scented the air with their perfume. Distractedly, Sophia dropped bits of sausage into the open mouth of Mr. Darcy, who was sitting at her feet.

"MMF."

This time, the exclamation was impossible to ignore. Sophia raised quizzical eyes at Lady Jane, who was going through the post received the day before.

Her aunt was shaking vigorously the missive she had in her hand, as if in the hope that the letters covering it would be reorganized by magic to form a new message more attuned to her mood.

"Dear child, you'll never guess who is getting married."

Pausing for dramatic effect, Lady Jane sipped some tea and patted the corners of her lips. Grimacing, she indicated the teapot to the maid who had entered carrying a dish of fruit with cream, and came back shortly with a fresh, steaming pot. Lady Jane waited until she had been served again before she dropped:

"Mathieu de Longchamp."

Sophia felt a pang somewhere not far from her stomach. In an instant, her toast with pheasant terrine lost its flavour.

"And who is the lucky woman?" she asked in a steady voice.

"Geraldine Cornell."

At the name, Sophia saw in her mind a young girl with pink cheeks, bright eyes, and teeth already bad, dressed all in white, a perfect replica of dozens of young girls who had been presented to Her Majesty that year.

"We are cordially invited," resumed Lady Jane, this time using a falsely official and high-pitched voice, "to celebrate the announcement of the happy event at an afternoon reception to take place Thursday week at the home of the future bride's parents, 14 Park Lane. I can reply right away that unfortunately we are otherwise engaged but that we offer the young couple our best wishes . . . ?" The interrogation was strictly for the sake of form. Obviously, her niece would have no desire to attend that reception. The mere fact of inviting her to it constituted a transgression of taste difficult to forgive.

To her own surprise, however, Sophia heard a voice that was hers reply: "No, Aunt, let us go. I shall be pleased to see Geraldine again." Then she took a sip of scalding tea and very nearly burned her tongue.

13 August 1846

FOR A WEEK we have been preparing to weigh anchor. The creak of the offshore ice, which is fissuring in the open sea, sometimes keeps us awake all night. It sounds as if a large animal were unfolding its numb limbs as it woke up. Crevices are beginning to form around the ships and we shall have to be careful that the chunks of ice, once they are separated, do not collide with or crush the hulls, which, although reinforced with steel, cannot withstand such assaults.

The tarpaulins covering the decks have been removed, the masts put up again, the sails, which are deeply creased and musty-smelling from their stay in the hold, have been smoothed out. We leave behind us a shoreline strewn with rubbish, the sole trace of our stay in an immaculate desert which soon will be covered with the snows of autumn. We must make haste as soon as the way is free, and clear ourselves a road towards the west through the growlers. We will perhaps finally have the opportunity to test the powerful locomotive motors of which Sir John was so proud and that to date have been of no use at all to us.

It is without regret that I shall leave this desolate winter and go back to sea; it, in one way or another, is always alive.

18 September 1846
69° 6' N, 102° 23' W, 17° F

Take careful note of Today's Date.

This historic day shall be inscribed in our Memories: after 8 days spent navigating Peel Sound, we caught sight today of the point of King William's Land, to the west of which opens the Passage, and we shall penetrate it in the Days to come.

All is well on Board. Morale is good.

Franklin sighed. Decidedly, he took no pleasure from writing, felt that he could never find the correct tone. The enthusiasm he was trying to express was not feigned but it was slightly premature, for it was possible that the maps indicating the mouth of the aforementioned passage might be as unreliable as the ones that he had had to rectify since the start of the voyage, some of which contained gross errors. Peel Sound itself was hardly sketched on most of the charts, which moreover depicted King William's Land as an indistinct mass with vague outlines.

It was obvious that to date no one had ever carried out a systematic reconnaissance of the region. Crozier had in fact suggested the ships sail around the headland towards the east so as to map methodically the coastlines, but Franklin had given him to understand that they had no time to waste plunging into a cul-de-sac while the Passage was doubtless within their reach.

"But perhaps, precisely, it is not a cul-de-sac," ventured Crozier. "The only maps showing the isthmus that joins this land to the rest of the mainland are riddled with errors."

"As far as I can see, my dear Crozier, you have taken on the mission of redrawing the Arctic entirely by yourself? Very well, I should not want to stand in your way, but if you have no objection, let's first find the Passage which is the reason for this expedition, before undertaking any ambitious cartographic project."

Sir John had uttered those last words with the good-natured chuckle that made the majority of his officers see him as a kind of bland uncle but which Crozier had learned to decipher as the sign of an irrevocable refusal. He had insisted, however, for if Sir John was unaware of the dangers that lay in wait for the ships farther west, Crozier had been notified of the threat by John Ross, who had warned him specifically about the huge masses of ice which, seeming to come down directly from the North Pole, piled up with unprecedented violence in this strait where Franklin was preparing to launch the *Erebus* and the *Terror*. He went so far as to show Sir John the description of this dangerous phenomenon that Ross had put in his logbook:

The pack of ice, which in the autumn of that year had been pressed against the shore, consisted of the heaviest masses that I have ever seen in such a situation. With this phenomenon, the lighter floes had been cast up on some parts of the coast in a most extraordinary and incredible manner, turning up large quantities of the shingle before them and in some places having travelled as much as half a mile beyond the limits of the highest tide-mark.

Franklin was not moved in the least. "You, dear Crozier, are not accustomed to these travel stories. You must know, however, that while the essentials of what is recounted in them are true, it happens that a need is felt to embellish the events somewhat or to make them appear more dreadful than in fact they are. I myself, while I am most rigorous, have occasionally . . . But stop worrying now, we shall be back in England in time for the new year."

And so, unaware of the strait between Somerset Island and King William's Land, the *Erebus* set sail towards the west, in accordance with the orders of Sir John Barrow, who, incidentally, spent that autumn day in 1846 at his club, where he lunched on a cutlet, potatoes, and peas.

21 September 1846

THERE ARE MORE and more ice floes; they drift slowly, sometimes turn, then come back and crash together. Virtually no water can be seen between the jagged slabs, greyish white in colour, that threaten to hold the ship in a tight embrace which it might well not survive. It is especially hazardous to clear one's way through this shifting labyrinth, and the ice masters have a great deal to do to keep the *Terror* and the *Erebus* out of danger. The two vessels advance almost one behind the other, the first opening the way for the second. It is now necessary to find a safe place where we can wait for another winter to end.

Sir John obstinately refuses to abandon even one of the steel cylinders that we loaded on by the hundreds, and during heavy weather we can hear their metallic cacophony in the hold. This despite the fact that it had been agreed we would jettison dozens at a time after we had inscribed the position of the ships as well as the general progress of the expedition on copies of a document requesting, in five languages, that whoever finds it be so kind as to dispatch it to the British government or to one of its emissaries or representatives.

When I reminded him that the cylinders were valuable tools enabling anyone who found them to follow our progress, or even, should it be necessary, to retrace the route we had taken, he replied cryptically: "Indeed. Precisely." Then he repeated, "Precisely. Precisely," as if he had just proved some irrefutable truth, after which he agreed to explain his reasoning:

"If we sow those cylinders without thinking, who can guarantee that they won't fall into the wrong hands? Who can prevent the first Russian ship, should it discover them, from attempting to catch up with us or even to pass us? You must know that we are not alone in seeking the Northwest Passage and that our rivals share neither our scruples nor our sense of honour." As he spoke those words, he looked extremely self-satisfied. I was speechless. Sir John is knowingly depriving us of the sole means of communication that we have for fear that our messages will be intercepted, as in some adventure novel. That explains at least why he was opposed to erecting a cairn on Beechey Island. And if those cylinders and the documents they contain are our sole means of communication, it does not mean, so far as I know, that they are in fact effective. Some of the tubes dropped by explorers' ships have been found seven years after they were entrusted to the sea, in the unlikeliest spots on the globe. For it is undeniable that those steel cylinders are very small, even if they are thrown into the water by the dozen, and the ocean is very big. Had we dropped one every day since our departure it is unlikely that even one would have been recovered, but it struck me as no less stupefying that Sir John would contravene deliberately the express orders of the Admiralty – to say nothing of plain common sense – lest the title Discoverer of the Northwest Passage should be stolen from him.

As I took my leave I went to look for one of those damned cylinders, which I took to my cabin. There, I extricated the sheet of paper that was rolled up inside it and on it wrote today's date, our position, and the route that we planned to follow. I closed up the tube and went on deck with the intention of throwing it overboard, half from defiance and half from a strange sense of duty or necessity, but I could not carry it out.

I went back down to my cabin in search, God help me, of something attractive. Alas, I had only her portrait, which it would be ridiculous to send to her and from which I refuse to be separated. My belongings are unimaginably dull and without ornament. I am certain that Fitzjames's drawers are overflowing with signet rings that have been passed on in his family from generation to generation as well as cufflinks set with precious stones, but for my part I possess nothing by way of jewels but my father's watch, which was given me when he died and is too bulky to be inserted into the thin cylinder that, in any case, it would cause to sink.

Eventually, for want of anything better, I pulled a brass button off my tunic and scrawled a hasty note which said:

> Kindly take this message in memory of me to Miss Sophia Cracroft, 21 Bedford Place, London. Let her keep it until the day of my return as I keep her picture in my mind.

I closed the cylinder and went back up on deck. A gibbous moon emerged from behind the clouds, casting silver ribbons onto the shifting surface of the waves. I hurled the cylinder, which struck the water with a faint sound and seemed to be floating in place while we continued to advance. Then I went back down to my cabin to sew a button onto my tunic, at once ashamed and happy.

THAT MORNING SOPHIA dressed with particular care, choosing a silk dress with shimmering highlights of pearl grey, sky blue, and rose and trimmed with a narrow edge of lace, only after she had considered carefully and then rejected everything that hung in her wardrobe. She fastened to her ears two delicate mother-of-pearl earrings set in silver and, around her neck, a pendant with a cameo presumed to depict Helen of Troy, whose profile it had been said resembled her own. She powdered the tip of her nose and applied a rose balm to her lips, then she perfumed herself not with bergamot, her everyday scent, but with magnolia. These operations completed, she brought her face close to the mirror on her dressing table to judge the result; she examined herself with satisfaction. With one finger she curled a lock of hair that had escaped from her studiedly negligent coiffure and used thumb and forefinger to pull out a white hair she had just discovered. Then she smiled and set off to celebrate the betrothal of Mathieu de Longchamp and Geraldine Cornell.

Nothing had been done by halves. No effort had been spared to mark the occasion fittingly. The Cornells' salons and parlour were overflowing with flowers sent by the cream of London society. In one corner, a chamber orchestra exuded soft music; on pedestal tables were arranged platters of meringues and macaroons; liveried servants offered the guests refreshments of all kinds; and in the conservatory a long table had been set up on which, among the bouquets of fresh flowers, confections and petits fours had been set out around a portrait of the young couple.

"My dears, I am delighted to see you both!"

The voice that welcomed them belonged not to the fiancée – who could not, for the moment, be seen – but to her mother, a rather corpulent, red-faced creature, with the quiet confidence of one who knows that she is a direct descendant of one of the oldest families in England but nonetheless is pleased to entertain at home, as equals, recently ennobled ladies and their plebeian nieces.

"Jane, you look radiant. And you, dear Sophia, are even more charming than I remember."

As the only occasion on which Sophia had had the honour of meeting Lady Cornell was a day when she had just arrived home after travelling a mile in the rain, finally pushing open the door with a sigh of relief, her nose red, hair dripping, dress sodden and smeared with mud, to find Lady Cornell in the foyer preparing to leave after a visit with Lady Jane, the compliment was not particularly generous.

"You're too kind," Sophia replied simply, smiling graciously.

"You know my daughter Geraldine, of course," Lady Cornell went on, turning to find the young woman among the crowd of guests, beckoning her to join them. Watching her approach, Sophia realized that her memory had played a trick on her. Geraldine Cornell was not that girl dressed all in white, with blue eyes and pink cheeks, whom she had spotted in the crowd of debutantes two years earlier: she was another, nearly identical, with a complexion equally fresh, with curls the same light brown, with eyes just as blue, and, as Sophia noted when the young girl smiled at her guests, with equally bad teeth.

During the week before the party, Sophia had prepared herself for all eventualities – most often unconsciously, while she stood at the window watching the rain fall, waiting for her aunt to go out, or soaking in her bath scented with orange blossom; sometimes even in a dream or during that half-sleep when one's thoughts follow one another with no apparent intervention by the brain, where they open and unfurl. She had pictured herself being introduced to Mathieu de Longchamp, smiling faintly as she whispered that she had already had the pleasure of meeting him, or leaving him to set the person straight while she remained silent, her head tipped slightly to one side, looking barely amused. She had imagined herself seeing him in the crowd by chance and greeting him either like an old, dear friend whom one scolds nicely for not having stayed in touch, or like some ordinary individual whose name one has trouble recalling but with whom one is cordial because good manners demand it.

The only thing she had not anticipated was that she would not see him – or, more precisely, that *he* would not see *her*. Over the two hours that Lady Jane Franklin and her niece, Sophia Cracroft, spent at the home of Lady Columbia Cornell to celebrate the betrothal of her daughter, Geraldine, Sophia:

- greeted 17 of her aunt's women friends and 32 gentlemen friends;

- had her hand kissed by 8 young men, one of whom – either he had not shaved very closely that morning or he was endowed with particularly vigorous facial hair –

grazed unpleasantly her white skin, which was scented with sweet almond oil;

➳ drank 1 glass of lemonade and 1 cup of tea;

➳ offered her compliments to the blushing young fiancée;

➳ ate 3 sandwiches and 2 meringues;

➳ drank another lemonade followed by a glass of seltzer;

➳ promised her friends Ursula and Amelia that she would accompany them to a charitable evening in aid of orphans;

➳ freshened up and, under the pretext of combing her hair and powdering her nose, went to the newly installed water closet to relieve herself;

➳ found herself alone and idle for 8 long minutes, forced to pretend that she was looking for her aunt until one of the young men mentioned above (no, not the one with the prickly beard, thank God, but another, one who was afflicted – no one is perfect – with very bad breath) came to discreetly court her;

➳ pretended to listen to the ramblings of old Miss Whitfield, who, having mistaken Sophia for her mother, insisted on asking about some ladies Sophia had never heard of and of whom, incidentally, a certain number had unfortunately passed away;

➳ while still pretending to be looking for her aunt in the crowd, knowing perfectly well that she was in the greenhouse admiring the collection of African violets that were Lady Cornell's pride and joy, tried to spot

Mathieu de Longchamp, wondering if she would recognize him immediately when she saw him from the back or heard his laughter.

In the end she did not have to make too great an effort because, along with his fiancée and her mother, he mounted a small podium set up for that purpose near the string quartet, which fell silent, and thanked the guests for coming to celebrate the happy occasion with them, and his future mother-in-law for having received him so graciously into the family that would soon be his.

He swept the room with his eyes as he spoke those few words without fixing his gaze on Sophia or even making her out among the faces turned his way. After which she:

🕊 went into the garden, where she took a few steps and then scurried back because it had started to rain;

🕊 had a very animated conversation and laughed a great deal with the young man afflicted with bad breath, who was in other respects charming;

🕊 began to suffer a slight headache behind her right eye;

🕊 did not refuse a drop of port wine.

WHILE LADY JANE takes a few steps in the garden with Sophia — whose pallor and lack of enthusiasm over the past two or three days have her worried — breathing in the aroma of the dead leaves that crackle beneath their feet, she tries to imagine that at the other end of the Earth it is already winter and night. While she *knows* rationally and could even explain the phenomenon of the Polar night to those who do not understand it, it still is hard for her to accept. She who has travelled — on foot, by boat, by mule or camel — Europe, North America, and almost all of Tasmania has no trouble envisaging the distance that separates her from her husband. What is difficult, virtually impossible even, is not to give in to the illusion that Sir John is also in some mysterious way remote in time. Her scientific mind rebels before that impression, though she senses that it is partly true.

At her side, Sophia is holding in her fingers a slender branch of willow from which she absent-mindedly strips the leaves. Lady Jane shakes herself to get rid of her unpleasant thoughts just as she would disperse a swarm of flies and grips her niece's elbow.

"Dear child," she says, "you've been very silent these past few days. What's wrong?"

"Nothing at all, Aunt. I've been thinking, that's all."

Then, despite herself, as if she'd only been waiting for this:

"The Cornells' party was a great success, wasn't it?"

Here it comes, thinks Lady Jane, while a kind of fatigue steals over her.

"Very much so," she replies. "I didn't have a chance to talk at any length with young Geraldine. What did you think of her?"

She waits.

"Well," declares Sophia steadily, carefully enunciating her syllables, "she is utterly charming. A milky complexion, exquisite manners, a voice like honey, a touch shy perhaps, which is quite normal at her age."

Lady Jane squeezes her niece's elbow and gives the young woman a sidelong glance before observing in a perfectly serious manner: "You would not have spoken differently to describe a piece of nougat. But you're right. Something about that young girl beguilingly calls to mind dessert; now that I reflect on her, I cannot help thinking of a plum pudding."

"Or a mincemeat pie," Sophia goes her one better.

"Or a sausage," concludes the aunt, and the two women continue along their way, smiling.

When she first came to the Franklins some twelve years earlier, Sophia, who was then a very young girl, was of course impressed by her legendary, larger-than-life uncle. But her relations with the hero whom fate had given her as a relative had soon proved to be rather limited, for highly intimidated by young women (especially when they were as pretty as his niece), he avoided as much as he could speaking to her or even meeting her gaze, contenting himself with the most rudimentary conversations. Had she slept well? Yes? Splendid. No? Most unfortunate. Would she like to accompany him and Lady Jane to the opera, where *The Marriage of Figaro* would be performed? Yes? Splendid.

Sophia's admiration had soon been transferred to Lady Jane, whose energy, sense of initiative, fighting spirit, and intelligence, qualities that would have seemed remarkable in a man, struck her as absolutely staggering in a woman, especially one who was so frail as well. It had been a revelation to young Sophia, who had been brought up between an incurably mundane mother whose sole concern was the proper running of her household and who measured her success by the perfection of her home's interior and of her domestics, for whom the apotheosis of the week was the serving of the midday meal on Sunday, and a neurasthenic aunt, an old maid who spent her days reading pious stories and embroidering. Between roast beef and petit-point, Sophia had refused to choose and she had won from her father the right to spend a summer at the home of her illustrious uncle, whose exploits she had read about in the newspapers.

Summer had given way to autumn, then to winter. One spring had blossomed, then another, and there was no longer any question of Sophia's going back to her parents. Lady Jane had no children, and her relations with Eleanor had never been a source of anything but renewed disappointment. She was incapable of understanding that exquisitely polite little girl whose serenity and impassivity were never disturbed but who seemed to her as devoid of inspiration and life as a stone. Even in her very early childhood, Eleanor never got carried away. She never shouted, never ran, never got dirty. Impervious to both reprimands and compliments, she made slow but regular progress in her education, attributable more to effort than to an inclination or a talent for any particular subject. She had become a secretive adolescent, shy and awkward, blushing for no reason at all, who rejected fiercely her stepmother's attempts to brighten up her way of dressing or to make her exchange her schoolgirl's plaits for a more stylish coiffure.

In Sophia Cracroft, then, Lady Jane had discovered the daughter she had never had but whom it was perhaps not too late to educate and mould, for her niece was endowed with a curiosity that was equalled only by her quick-wittedness, and the niece had discovered in her uncle's wife the model she had been missing since her earliest childhood: a brilliant, independent woman capable, if necessary, of standing up to the entire world.

Sophia was convinced that Lady Jane herself would have been an exceptional explorer. By way of confirmation she had only to read the journals her aunt had kept during her travels, where she noted methodically the distances travelled, the geographical accidents observed, the temperatures recorded, as well as providing descriptions at once precise and inspired of places visited and populations encountered. Once, Sophia had even started to collect the journals that her aunt had written during her journeys to Egypt and Tasmania, with the intention of retranscribing them and entrusting them to a publisher. Lady Jane had protested half-heartedly, then offered to let her niece consult as well the letters she had written during those same journeys – of which, astutely, she had preserved the rough drafts.

3 November 1846

YESTERDAY MORNING the propellers were lifted, to be placed in
the hold where they will stay until the pack ice melts, then the
vessels were hoisted onto the ice, which is solid enough that it
is not liable to crush the ships once spring arrives. The men,
who have been given a supplementary ration of rum along with
strict instructions to wear their warmest clothing, went out
onto the ice as joyfully as children about to build a snowman.
The cables attached to various places on the *Terror* were flung
onto the ice and the men took hold of them to set about hauling
the enormous wooden carcass. Standing on the deck, armed with
a speaking tube, Gore bellowed rhythmically, Heave ho! which
was met each time by a slight movement forward by the ship,
emerging from the icy water like a sea monster wrenched away
from its natural habitat. For a second I had the impression that
I was seeing come to life before my eyes one of those ancient
engravings depicting slaves sentenced to Roman galleys, except
that these prisoners, driven off the ship, were forced to make
it advance in a manner even more punishing. Once the *Terror*
was entirely out of the ice, it became easier to slide it across
several hundred feet, to a spot where it was relatively sheltered
from the wind, before an enormous wave of ice that seemed to
have risen up on the icefield over the centuries like a mountain
of frozen water. It was past two o'clock in the afternoon; the
men, drenched by their efforts, no longer felt the cold, though
it was biting. They were served a hot stew along with a fresh

ration of rum, after which they had to do it all again in order to hoist the *Erebus* beside the *Terror*. Fatigue, the dark – the sun had long since disappeared from the horizon and all that remained was a greyish glow in the sky that erased every colour on Earth – limbs numb from alcohol and cold, the accidents multiplied. One sailor broke his hand; two others, sliding across the ice, suffered nasty sprains; not to mention the fact that two of the cables snapped, and they had to readjust others countless times to avoid damaging the ship, which, submitted to torque or poorly balanced pressure, was letting out worrisome creaks. It was well past midnight when the men could finally go back on board and get into their bunks after being seen by Peddie, who wanted to be sure that no one was suffering from overly severe chilblains or any other injuries that had gone unnoticed. After more rum had been poured, the order was issued this one time, on both boats, to keep the heat on all night. This morning there are countless red or purplish noses, chins as white as flour, earlobes blackened by cold. Winter has imposed on the crew a grim carnival makeup.

EVERY DAY THE deck must be scrubbed until it shines not like a new penny – money is of no use in this small, isolated Arctic society at the end of the Earth – but so that the skirts of a lady wearing a white gown could sweep it without being soiled. That lady in white is with the men in thought while they work their fingers to the bone, on all fours, hands chapped and blue from the cold, knees scraped by their heavy woollen trousers which are constantly freezing and thawing, backs exhausted by the burden of their constant labour. She floats above them, light, graceful, elusive. No doubt they make out her evanescent silhouette in the cloud of mist that escapes from their mouths and disperses in front of them before it forms again with the next exhalation, or else they spy her in a dream then see her disappear at dawn, a white shadow tangled with the black of night.

Once the job is done, the shivering men go back inside until the next day, the snow slips through chinks in the canvas stretched above the deck and comes back to dance on the wood – light, graceful, elusive.

WHITE, AS FAR AS the eye can see. The white of the sky which merges with the white of the earth buried under the snow, which melts into the white of the water covered with ice, which melts into the white that ends up inside tired eyelids when eyes are closed.

A grey white under clouds heavy with snow, a shadow white that swallows up distances and deceives the pupils of our eyes. A white veil that covers everything.

A black white on sunless winter days.

Translucent and veiled, impenetrable, aqueous and solid, spotless, the opposite of all stains. A white like an eye, which at the same time masks and reveals what is found behind, beneath, beyond.

A bluish white that glitters in the light of the enormous, swollen moon and in the light of the millions of stars sparkling on the snow where they seem to be reflected or to have fallen to Earth.

The yellow white of the pack ice where seals crawl and the fields of snow where we relieve ourselves and empty the chamber pots.

The ashen white of moonless nights which last sometimes for weeks.

Everywhere, white. A little way off, the spittle of a sailor, like a red star on the snow.

Perlerorneq. That is the word the Esquimaux use for the feeling that eats away at the hearts of men during the winter that stretches out endlessly, when the sun seldom appears. *Perlerorneq*. Hoarse as the lament of an animal that senses the approach of death.

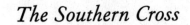

The Southern Cross

ON THIS CHRISTMAS DAY, the men have been exempted from chores, aside from those who work in the galley and enjoy embellishing their everyday fare and that of their workmates. They have cooked thirty sweet breads with dried fruits which, soaked in rum, taste a little like plum pudding and recall for all of them the Christmases of their childhood, when snow was an eagerly anticipated gift and not a prison; other dishes to be served include mashed potatoes (prepared with the last of the shrivelled, greenish tubers that are moulding in the hold, but are nonetheless fresh vegetables) to accompany the tinned stew from Mr. Goldner, its flavour enhanced with clove and nutmeg.

At the Captain's table are seated the usual men: Crozier, Fitzjames, DesVoeux, Peddie, Gore, Sargent. From below decks, where the men are being served double rations of grog and of food, joyous shouts can be heard. In the officers' mess, however, all are silent, as if they were at table with strangers. Just as the champagne is about to be opened, Sir John rises to deliver the speech he has prepared:

"I am happy to be spending a new Christmas in your company. Consider, my friends, that we are writing History. We have almost achieved our goal and soon the Night shall rise to make room for a new Day. And that day shall be the day of our Discovery and our Victory. England will know how to thank her Sons, my friends, who will have offered . . ."

He interrupts himself, no longer certain about what he has composed, regrets having left the sheet on which he has written the lines in his cabin. He repeats to himself, in a low voice, " . . . who will have offered her . . ." then, taking the plunge, concludes emphatically: " . . . a New Continent." Though somewhat surprised, the guests applaud politely.

Curiously, throughout this meal, taken in the ice of Peel Sound, Crozier recalls not happy Christmas Days spent with his family — as he has spent the bulk of his adult life at sea, those Christmases were not so numerous — but December 25 the year before, when all were still enthusiastic, impatient, feverish at the thought of the discoveries to come. It seemed that this energy, having no object to grapple with, had turned against the very ones who had nourished it, to devour them from inside. Their faces are gaunt, bloodless, of a dull, thick whiteness that is reminiscent of dough. Their eyes shine with an unhealthy brilliance. Some of the men are speechless for days, then start to laugh with no one to silence them. Others weep silently, tears running onto their faces before disappearing inside their greyish collars. All, however, have close-shaven cheeks, hair cut short to prevent infestations of lice and fleas — a useless precaution, for the insects are everywhere, not just in their hair but in the blankets and sheets, on the rats that can be heard scratching in the dark, in the secrecy of armpits and groins, in woollen clothing, and even in the folds of the flags that have been brought to plant where they would take possession of the territory in the name of the Crown. Laundry is done once a month, in the enormous vats that are used for preparing food and are filled for the occasion with boiling, soapy water. This treatment has worn out the fabrics and the colours, all now verging on grey.

One morning, a sailor who was using an axe to try opening a fifty-pound tin of food cut his leg badly. Rather than come to his aid, the dozen or so men around him stood there as if petrified at the sight of the blood spurting steadily from the wound. Crozier himself, taken aback, had to force himself to surmount the fascination that had overcome him, sling the injured man over his shoulder, and take him to Peddie. Reflecting on the incident, he realized it was the first time in weeks that he'd seen a straightforward colour that had not been faded by wear, water, salt, wind. That night when he was falling asleep he struggled to recall all the red things he could think of and imagine in the slightest detail their hues and their subtleties, like a man who has gone too long without talking, and fearing that he will become mute recites to himself the nursery rhymes of his childhood.

The first strawberries of spring, coral speckled with the gold of their tiny seeds; tulips of vermilion satin; blood on the sheets in the morning when, still nearly a child, he had shared his bed with a young servant girl who slipped in beside him at nightfall; the first tomatoes of summer with their pinkish, acid flesh; poppies, orange around their black hearts; the shutters on his grandmother's house, wine-coloured but faded now;

cherries of a deep and velvety crimson; the red red of the cross of Saint George on the Union Jack that had floated from the mast of the *Terror* on the day of their departure; the guts of the rabbits he'd caught in a snare as a child, purplish pink shot through with veins.

The mouth of Sophia Cracroft.

THE YEARS SPENT in Tasmania had been difficult for Sophia. The penal colony offered few distractions. There were neither museums nor theatres, no pastry shop worthy of the name, and the countryside was crawling with snakes. (In an attempt to suppress the population, Lady Jane had offered a reward to anyone who brought her one of the horrible creatures dead, but the venture had to be abandoned shortly afterwards, for the reptilian remains were piling up in the courtyard of the governor's house and her budget was melting away, while the number of snakes nearby seemed undiminished.) Unlike her aunt, Sophia had no passion for the rehabilitation of dangerous criminals or for the education of poor women, victims of circumstance, or for the instruction of children born either to the former or the latter; nor was she burning to put into practice various theories gleaned from works of philosophy and politics. If the colony was for Lady Jane a vast laboratory, Sophia saw it more as a vast open-air jail in which she herself was an innocent prisoner. She had never enjoyed the presence of girls her age very much, so the absence of companions other than her aunt did not weigh on her, although she would have liked to be able to go out in society now and then, to dance and flutter her fan for a few moments next to a young admirer before going back to whirl around again.

When James Clark Ross and Francis Rawdon Moira Crozier, along with their crews, made a stop at Hobart on their way to Antarctica after sailing virtually around the world on the *Terror* and the *Erebus*, weeks had gone by since the governor and his circle had seen new faces. The explorers were received with great pomp, as the heroes they would be some months later, as soon as they were back in the mother country.

Of the two captains, Ross was the more handsome, of that there was no doubt, the more amiable, too. Crozier, though, was not without a certain allure; on all occasions he demonstrated a calm self-confidence, and in his presence other men always looked more or less like little boys. He had a square face, firm, nearly impassive features, deep-set dark eyes that in an instant might come alive and shine with a brilliance that could have been due to happiness or to the fire of a muffled anger. On top of all that, he was a redhead. Most often he spoke with effort, his voice low and words carefully chosen; unlike so many other young officers, he did not know how to coo sweet nothings into a lady's ear.

Among the few young girls in the colony, a very small number—four—were unmarried, and none had a waist so slender, eyes so velvety, a smile so winning as Sophia, who became the subject of many poems praising her beauty and her wit.

As for Sophia, she let herself be lulled by these praises spoken by a hundred mouths as if by a sea with calm, warm water. It was as if a single large, adoring creature, Her Majesty's Navy, was paying tribute to her. Choosing one suitor would have meant forsaking all others, extracting him from the group of comrades. Because each was in a sense the reflection of all those around him, because they multiplied and glorified one another, the group was in fact what truly interested her. What woman would settle for a captain when the entire Admiralty bowed to her?

And so Sophia discovered that she was lighter than she had ever been in England, where – leaving aside a brief idyll with Mathieu de Longchamp, who, after two or three kisses, had undertaken to persuade Sophia to give him her hand, which had marked the end of their relationship, nor had she responded to any of the letters he had addressed to Hobart – she had always been careful to behave in all circumstances with full propriety. In the Antipodes she, of course, did not stop conforming scrupulously with the rules of decorum, but she allowed herself a few smiles, a few stolen looks, a few languid poses. For most of the men, deprived of the company of the fair sex for months, these represented the very essence of femininity, a portent of the fiancée or the wife with whom they would be reunited, or had yet to meet, on their return.

For Crozier, however, they were more.

When the two captains came back five months later, Crozier – whose hair now had more silver threads than gold ("A single night in Antarctica did that," he said laconically to Lady Jane, then never referred to it again) – had decided to make Sophia his wife.

To thank their hosts for the gracious welcome they had been given, and also to celebrate the fact that they were nearing the end of a perilous expedition that had lasted for more than four years, the two captains had organized a grand ball on the *Erebus* and the *Terror* for the leading members of Hobart society.

The two ships had been arranged so that their hulls touched and were chained together so as to form a single vessel. Access was by a footbridge made of dozens of rowing boats fixed to one another, decorated with pennants and mimosa, the floral symbol of the island, which scented the air with its sweet perfume. The topsides of the *Erebus* had been fitted out as the ballroom, while on the deck of the *Terror* tables overflowing with superior foodstuffs and the finest wines in the governor's cellar had been set up. A white cloth canopy reminiscent of a lost sail or the protective wing of some enormous bird had been hung above the two decks, which accommodated three hundred hand-picked guests, all delighted with these maritime festivities.

In the midst of all their pomaded, perfumed, close-shaven men wearing clean and freshly starched uniforms, the two captains looked like the two sovereigns of a small nautical dominion.

The evening was mild, the atmosphere nearly magical on board the two ships swaying gently on the waters of Hobart Bay. Sophia Cracroft had never enjoyed herself so much. Champagne flowed freely, and she did not miss a waltz, changing partners at every dance, whirling in the moonlight. On all the walls hung mirrors that reflected the brilliance of the candles; in them she could catch a glimpse, repeated a hundred times, of her own face with its pink cheeks and its shining eyes.

Dancing with John Ross, she sank into his arms for a moment, almost expecting to feel herself lifted up, floating above the deck, so light and sylphlike did she feel. The Captain, worried, caught hold of her and suggested that she take some fresh air for a moment. Politely, she assented.

In the bow of the ship, the sounds of the party were somewhat muffled, distorted by the reverberation stamped on them by the movement of the waves as they licked the hull. Stars dotted the black water with a thousand dancing points of light.

A slight breeze was blowing from the sea and Sophia shivered. Ross took off his jacket and placed it around the shoulders of the young woman, who shuddered again. Looking at the sky sprinkled with so many lights that it seemed almost milky, she asked him in a fluty voice if he knew all the stars. He shrugged:

"No, not all of them, far from it. I know the sailors' stars. There is, umm, the Southern Cross, that helps you find the celestial South Pole by following the line formed by Crux and Gacrux."

He pointed to the sky, where millions of twinkling stars seemed to Sophia's eyes absolutely identical.

"Where is that?"

"Right there, below Centaurus. It's the smallest constellation in the sky."

"Could we begin with something easier, then? A constellation that is visible? I thought that they were all named for the gods and heroes of mythology who went into battle for the charms of irresistible nymphs and naiads afflicted with jealous husbands."

"Yes, of course, a great many of these constellations were discovered by the Ancients, who gave them the names of their gods. But I fear that I know the stories less than their usefulness for navigators when it is time to take one's bearings . . ."

Sophia sighed in the face of such dull pragmatism. They were alone beneath a sky that could have been studded with diamonds, being gently lulled by the waves in Hobart Bay and the distant harmonies of the orchestra that were coming on the wings of a gentle wind scented with magnolia – and here she was with this deuced Captain who could only talk about navigation. She kept an irritated silence.

"You'll excuse me, dear Sophia, but I must go back to my

duties as host," he announced after a moment. He kissed her hand, bowed to her slightly as if she were some dowager, then turned on his heels.

Alone, leaning on the ship's rail, Sophia was hesitating between wrath, despondency, and laughter when Crozier appeared at her side. She was amused to note that he was trembling.

"Are you well?" he asked in an unsteady voice.

"Wonderfully well, thank you. I was simply a little warm over there. And then all those people were making me dizzy . . ."

"If you would rather be alone I can . . ."

"No, no, stay, it's fine. You can no doubt teach me a great many fascinating things about the proper use of stars in navigation."

He looked at her, taken aback.

Her voice softened. "Excuse me. I'm sometimes rather blunt."

They stood there stock-still for a long moment. She could hear him breathing at her side.

He began: "You must know that . . ." he stammered, "that Antarctica bears that name because it is at the polar opposite to the Arctic."

Sophia gave him a sidelong look.

"I had no idea," she declared. "But it seems to me quite appropriate."

Silence returned. Crozier felt a thin film of perspiration coat his palms.

"As for the Arctic," he went on, "it takes its name . . ."

"Wait, don't say another word, it owes its name to the fact that it is located at the polar opposite to Antarctica?"

Crozier smiled faintly. This was not at all the way he had

imagined their conversation. He was boring her with his geographical tales, that was obvious. But if he was silent now, all was lost. He resumed then, his voice nearly resigned: "That is a most interesting hypothesis but, alas, incorrect. The Arctic owes its name to the constellation of the Bear – Arktos – which looks down on it."

"Really?" said Sophia, whose interest had been aroused slightly. "A bear? And where is it?"

"Well, as we are, you see, at the Antipodes to the Arctic, that constellation is invisible from here."

"So we see different stars depending upon where we are on Earth?"

That notion, which had never brushed her mind, suddenly made her head spin. Really, you could trust nothing.

"No, the stars change . . . In fact it is we who change, but they are not the same . . ."

He broke off, unable to pursue an idea that had got inexplicably muddled. Whenever he was in Sophia's presence his thoughts became tangled, his hands damp, his tongue thick, and he knew himself a perfect idiot.

They were silent for a moment, she plunged in stunned contemplation of the starry sky, he transfixed by his own stupidity. Then, at the cost of a thousand efforts, he tried again:

"When I was small," he began without looking at her, "there were three books in our house: the Bible, a dog-eared almanac, and an old volume about astronomy picked up who knows where, with half its pages missing. And so, once I had learned how to recognize Orion, Cassiopeia, the Big and Little Dippers, I resolved to make up the rest. From my bedroom window under the eaves I could make out in the black sky the constellation of the Pig, the Hen, and the Ear of Corn. There were also Mr. Pincher, the village blacksmith with his crooked nose, the Owl, and the Commode."

Sophia could not stop herself from laughing.

"And tonight it seems to me that I can see a new constellation in the sky which I've never seen before, yet it includes the brightest star. Look, Sophia," he said, leaning gently against her and grasping her right hand to raise it to the level of their eyes, "do you see that very bright star in the midst of its paler neighbours? Follow my hand."

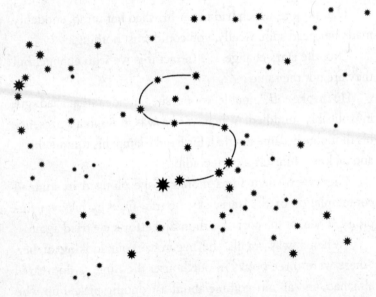

He seemed then to touch with his fingers eight stars, then he joined them together by drawing an *S* in the middle of the sky that appeared, after being thus designated, to shine with a more brilliant light.

Sophia allowed her head to rest against Crozier's shoulder. A warm wind enveloped them.

Then the second mate of the *Terror* appeared, out of breath, and announced to Crozier that Captain Ross was waiting for him to propose the toasts.

IN THE MIDST of a spotless, sterile landscape as white and vacant as the surface of the chalky Moon that casts an ashen light onto the snow, the bellies of the boats, warm, damp, nauseating, rest like the entrails of some sea monster washed onto shore. Dismasted, sitting slightly askew on the ice that holds them tightly like a vise, covered with tarpaulins intended to insulate them and make them easier to heat, the *Erebus* and the *Terror*, jewels of Her Majesty's Navy, look like dying whales, their bellies aswarm with a multitude of worms.

The damp air smells of coal, wet wool, sweat, and ammonia. Every particle that is inhaled has already passed through the galley, the engine room, the hold; it has already been breathed by a hundred other blocked noses, inhaled by healthy or tubercular lungs, exhaled by a hundred sour mouths. It has emerged in the form of a belch or flatulence with the sickly sweet smell that heralds dysentery. And in the midst of a desert of absolute whiteness, in the midst of waves of snow carved by the wind that blows over thousands of miles without encountering an obstacle, this contaminated air enters like a poisoned liqueur and emerges a little more foul, altered by its passing through a new body.

For these reasons it is good to go outside into the open air, despite the cold whose bite is so intense that one might think of a burn, despite the light of the sun which blinds the men. That is why the outside chores are distributed like rewards, and why, in spite of the risks, nearly everyone volunteers for reconnaissance expeditions.

23 March 1847

WE HAVE HAD TO STRIKE out the magnetic observations made over the past three months, for after a thousand verifications, they have proven to be incorrect, as if the instruments had been thrown out of order by some mysterious force. I questioned separately the men who took part in the last eight expeditions, and all swore that they followed the usual procedure to the letter. Moreover, as the composition of the teams varies from one foray to the next, it seems to me unlikely that one or more individuals should have knowingly altered the results without the others' knowledge. It goes without saying that the declination compasses as well as all the instruments have been taken apart so that their various components can be examined from every angle, following which they were assembled again and tested. All the readings obtained corresponded with those already noted. The problem then does not lie on that side. Until it is resolved, I have decided to suspend the expeditions.

— I HAVE NEVER SEEN so many stars at home. Why are there so many here, where there's no one to look at them?

— They're not more numerous. It's simply that we make them out better because for miles around there are no other lights to outshine them and dim their brilliance.

Suddenly, in the vast sky appears a milky green glimmering, a moving wave that dances above the horizon where it unfurls a shimmering, nearly phosphorescent curtain.

— Are these hidden by the city lights in London, too?

— No, these only exist here.

— Why is that?

— Perhaps because we're here to see them.

Thomas is silent for several minutes, absorbed in contemplating the celestial currents fringed with rose and rippling in the black velvet of the night. Then curiosity gets the upper hand.

— What are they?

— *Aurora borealis.* The Northern Lights.

Thomas repeats to himself this name, which seems to confirm to him that the place where he is, is at once at the end and the dawn of the world.

LADY JANE WAS well aware of the importance of maintaining good relations with the ladies of high society just as with the wives of various senior officials and dignitaries, never knowing who might prove to be useful for the fulfilment of her plans. Therefore, every Wednesday she invited to tea all who had invited her in the course of the preceding week but who had received by way of response a small card explaining that she regretted that she must decline but would be delighted to have them as her guests.

There were then some fifteen or twenty of these ladies who turned up at Bedford Place around four o'clock one afternoon, when the sun was descending over a city bathed in golden light. In front of her door stretched a long line of carriages, the coachmen waiting stoically for their mistresses who had gone inside to quench their thirst while the horses gently tapped the ground with their hooves.

Quickly relieved by Alice of their parasols and mantillas, they were greeted by Sophia, who led them to the sitting room where tea was served. Lady Jane had never been a woman to be content with little, and since this tea party was the showcase she was offering to the world, it had a duty to reflect her: surprising, bold, exotic, complex, and incomparable.

A samovar of finely worked silver had pride of place at the centre of the table; from it came an aroma of spices in which the more adventurous of her guests could recognize clove and cardamom. Other teapots held more discreetly the traditional Earl Grey, African red tea (a beverage that inspired a certain suspicion, in which the courageous who ventured to try it tasted a hint of brown sugar), and for delicate natures subject to palpitations, an infusion of pale camomile blossoms that floated on the surface of the steaming water.

Among the cheese scones and jam tarts, the shortbread and the sandwiches of bread sliced so thin that it was nearly diaphanous and allowed one to see the filling (egg, cucumber, salmon), Lady Jane was careful to scatter some exotic foods that reminded her guests – lest they had forgotten it for a moment – that they were enjoying the privilege of sharing this meal with the wife of one of the greatest explorers in the world: translucent Turkish delight scented with rose, mint, or pistachio and coated in icing sugar; fresh figs, imported at great expense, that had been roasted with a drop of alcohol or a hint of nutmeg; rose-coloured biscuits from the city of Reims that crunched when bitten into; Greek delicacies composed of a fragile assemblage of paper-thin sheets of pastry soaked in clover honey. Each of these strokes of inspiration was accompanied – and this was the goal of the display of tidbits – by a story that recounted its origin, the etymology of its name, or the first encounter between Lady Jane and the dish in question, under the desert sun or in the cool shadow of the walls of a medieval city. These ladies, even if they had never travelled farther than to her sitting room, would nonetheless have journeyed practically around the world.

In an armoire that held the place of honour were shelves on which the treasures from Lady Jane's travels were displayed. While the artifacts and sundry objects collected by her husband and his subalterns during his explorations sat imposingly and very visibly in the library, this showcase was devoted entirely to the fruits of her own peregrinations, and were all the more precious for having been discovered and arranged by her own hand, like a bouquet of rare flowers.

There, side by side, were a desert rose, the irregular harmony of whose delicate spines invariably roused the admiration of these ladies, though Lady Jane preferred not to reveal to them the source of such singular beauty; a dagger with a carved blade in a *repoussé* leather sheath, for which she had negotiated fiercely with one of the blue-clad men who smelled as strong as the camels whose existence they shared; a *grigri* made of horn, feathers, and onyx marbles that had always created in her a very slight anxiety; the perfectly preserved fossil of a flower on which the veined petals and even the small bristling hairs that covered the leaves with a coarse fuzz could be made out; a mosquito held prisoner in a large drop of honey-coloured amber, suspended for all eternity in its translucent gold; a sculpture that depicted with nearly obscene crudeness the silhouette of a woman with well-developed breasts and rounded hips (which the women pretended not to see for fear the others might imagine those same forms hiding beneath the petticoats, chemisettes, and crinolines they were decked out in themselves); gossamer figures in brightly coloured blown glass, purchased on the island of Murano, a concession granted by the adventurous lady to the fashion of the time, for the small figures, while silly and indeed quite common, were nonetheless the work of genuine artisans. Moreover, Lady Jane was fond of telling the history of the glass-blowers who had been relegated to that island because of fears that they might set fire to immortal Venice. The workshops of sand and fire set down in the middle of the lagoon struck her as a rather pretty image.

After duly admiring Lady Jane's collection of curiosities and the paintings that adorned her walls, the guests sat in armchairs upholstered in tapestry that depicted mythological scenes such as Diana hunting the stag and Io fleeing Zeus; they tasted the various sweets that were offered them, and soon a confused murmur filled the room, a combination of dozens of high-pitched and polite voices trying to be heard above the others. Gracefully, Lady Jane went from group to group, bestowing the same attention on each.

"What a magnificent gown. And the colour is ever so becoming."

"It is even worse than one might think, for her son-in-law became involved, and you can imagine what happened."

"A gem, I tell you. My sister who lives in Bath couldn't get over it."

"Incidentally, what did you tell him?"

"Not before dinner, thank you."

"And what would happen otherwise? Someone must have conducted the search to know to whom the inheritance would fall . . ."

"It's pistachio, I believe. I have trouble distinguishing among all these nuts."

"My dear, you have scored a bull's eye. But keep it to yourself, of course. Otherwise tongues might wag."

"And what is the name?"

"I assure you, I have invented nothing: a thousand pounds."

Lady Jane and Sophia emerged exhausted from these weekly receptions, their ears buzzing, their souls occupied by a profound sense of emptiness. Most often they went to bed without eating, and the servants had crustless sandwiches and pastries dripping with honey, enough for two days.

WITH THE RETURN of spring, Peddie went back to the herbarium for which he gathered leaves, flowers, mosses, seaweed, even the smallest twigs that poked their heads through the pebbles and gravel that covered the inhospitable soil of King William's Land. With a magnifying glass screwed into his eye, he devoted entire evenings to identifying his precious finds with the help of the numerous botany books in the library of the *Terror*, then meticulously arranging his specimens according to the family, genus, and species to which they belonged, writing their Latin and English names in a clear and scientific hand. Adam had been helping for a few weeks to classify and organize the specimens and to peruse the botany books in search of possible cross-references. When by chance the two, after exhaustive research, found nowhere in the books descriptions or illustrations corresponding to some plant they had collected or one that had been brought to them — for it goes without saying that anyone who left the ship invariably came back with some present for Peddie, the herbarium thereby becoming a collective project — Adam would christen it with the name of the crew member who had brought it to Peddie to be studied, or with the name of another with whom it seemed to him to share some physical or moral characteristic. Peddie saw nothing wrong with this so long as his assistant took care to inscribe, under the invented names, the factual elements they had been able to determine beyond any doubt. It had occurred to him recently that, fundamentally, most plant names had been similarly invented, but as that thought created a kind of malaise in him, he had chased it away at once.

And so the delicate *Draba nivalis*, which in winter raises tiny arms bearing oval, translucent capsules out of the snow, a small vegetable creature whose apparent fragility conceals a force comparable to that of the ice, silent and diaphanous, was given the name *Veronica*, in memory of a soft-voiced nun in the orphanage, as well as the boringly descriptive appellation *snow whitlow grass*. Similarly, on the wide, beige pages one saw next to the ranunculus, anemones, and *Aronia ovalis*, with its delicious fruit, some Hornby's Trumpets, MacDonald's Lilies, and Eliot's Bells, named for one or another of his companions.

Satisfied with the work of his young apprentice, Peddie suggested that he write a description of one of the plants just identified, the Arctic Willow. The young man had read enough of such writings, the surgeon considered, to be capable of replicating the structure. He himself would correct the inaccuracies that would no doubt slip into his work. The few lines that Adam turned in, however, left him deeply perplexed. The fine, elegantly formed letters, leaning slightly forward, themselves resembled the delicate stem of some simple with overly ornate flowers:

It would appear that the Arctic Willow belongs in equal measure to the animal and vegetable kingdoms, an unlikely cross between the Cherry and the Caterpillar. Completely covered with a silvery Down which resembles the coat of certain Arctic animals, the plant measures no more than a few inches in height but it stretches out in some cases across a surface several feet square. It bristles with bright

Red and Yellow antennæ, which end in a slight Swelling,
and are stuck into black, velvety scales. Overall it is rem-
iniscent of the Softness and the colour of the wings of a
Butterfly as foreshadowed by the Caterpillar.

Peddie had been obliged to reread the lines twice to assure himself that the young man had not mistakenly given him someone else's fable or a poem just for fun. Then he wondered if this Adam had meant to mock him as he endeavoured to carry out a serious scientific venture that had nothing to do with this . . . *literature.* Once he had named the thing that he was holding in his hands, he felt somewhat better and ready to confront his assistant. As a man of patience and persistence, he armed himself first with one of the descriptions of which he was proudest, one that struck him, because it was concise and precise, as a model of the kind, the one he had written for the purple saxifrage (*Saxifraga oppositifolia*).

Small low plant having a rose-fuchsia blossom with five
stamens (which are a vibrant yellow). Grows on rocky
soil where it forms a thick carpet, appears at the end of
June and disappears in September. Its smooth, deep green
leaves are most often packed tightly on their stems, but on
some specimens may be very widely spaced. Exceptionally
hardy, saxifrage is sometimes the only plant that will grow
in particularly infertile soil. It does not emit any aroma.

Next came a detailed Linnaean taxonomy whose subtleties he had not considered it necessary to explain to his young apprentice; that would have required, among other things, lessons in Latin, which he felt neither the wish nor the competence to undertake.

When Adam came back the next day to give him new specimens the men had collected, Peddie invited him to sit down and cleared his throat.

"I read what you gave me yesterday . . . It's . . . very fine . . . hmmm . . . But, you see, my lad, it's important to be more rigorous. We must note facts, objective observations . . ."

Adam interrupted him. He seemed slightly disappointed but not surprised.

He took from his pocket a paper folded in four.

"I didn't give you this yesterday because I was not absolutely certain about the sub-class . . . But I checked this morning, it does indeed belong to the *dilleniidæ*. Excuse me, I'm expected in the galley." And he left.

Unfolding the paper, Peddie saw, written in the same hand with fine upstrokes:

SALIX ARCTICA
Regnum: Plantæ
Subregnum: Tracheobionta
Phylum: Spermatophyta
Subphylum: Magnoliophyta
Classis: Magnoliopsida
Subclassis: Dilleniidæ
Ordo: Salicales
Familia: Salicaceæ
Genus: Salix

Incredulous, he took the book that he used for reference most often, a dog-eared catalogue with a leather cover crazed from too much handling, and began feverishly to consult it, as if he were hoping to discover a flaw in this taxonomical tree that he knew would turn out to be perfectly correct.

SOME DAYS AGO the men started building a cairn with the same energy they would have put into erecting a lighthouse or, if shipwrecked on a desert island, a raft on which they would hope to brave the waves. Sir John, who since the beginning of the expedition has been fiercely opposed to our leaving any useless sign of our passage, apparently does not have the heart to forbid their project. It must be said that we left the shore of Beechey Island littered with empty tins and various sorts of trash, as well as planting the three crosses that testify in silence to our time here. Perhaps he believes that, planted where they are, they render vain any attempt to pass unnoticed. Or perhaps he thinks rather that the cairn, located in a declivity a few hundred yards from the desolate shore, runs no risk of being seen.

All I know is that when Fitzjames came to make that request, he gave his consent straightforwardly. As the landscape is covered with a heavy layer of snow, it has taken a few days to gather the rocks needed to erect the tower, which is scarcely taller than a man. Into it was slipped one of the sheets of paper on which a message is typed in five languages, the same one that I cast pointlessly into the sea along with a button; Fitzjames wrote on it a few lines that Sir John read absent-mindedly, as if the contents were of no interest to him. He then held out the paper for me to read and I noted that it contained an error: we spent not the winter of 1846–1847 on Beechey Island, rather that of 1845–1846. Sir John and Fitzjames shrugged their shoulders, as if it were something inconsequential. I did not insist, for I have trouble imagining what use one could make of the message: as long as our ships are iced in not far away, they point out our presence, and once we have weighed anchor, it will point to the location that we occupied the year before and will, as a result, be absolutely null and void.

H. M. S. *ships* Erebus and Terror {Wintered in the Ice in

28 of May 1847 { Lat. 70° 5′ N. Long. 98° 23′ W

Having wintered in 1846—7 at Beechey Island
in Lat. 74° 43′ 28″ N. Long. 91° 39′ 15″ W. After having
ascended Wellington Channel to Lat. 77° and returned
by the West side of Cornwallis Island.

Commander.

John Franklin commanding the Expedition

All well

WHOEVER finds this paper is requested to forward it to the Secretary of
the Admiralty, London, *with a note of the time and place at which it was
found*: or, if more convenient, to deliver it for that purpose to the British
Consul at the nearest Port.

QUINCONQUE trouvera ce papier est prié d'y marquer le tems et lieu ou
il l'aura trouvé, et de le faire parvenir au plutot au Secretaire de l'Amirauté
Britannique à Londres.

CUALQUIERA que hallare este Papel, se le suplica de enviarlo al Secretarie
del Almirantazgo, en Londres, con una nota del tiempo y del lugar en
donde so halló.

EEN ieder die dit Papier mogt vinden, wordt hiermede verzogt, om het
zelve, ten spoedigste, te willen zenden aan den Heer Minister van de
Marine der Nederlanden in 's Gravenhage, of wel aan den Secretaris den
Britsche Admiraliteit, te London, en daar by te voegen eene Nota,
inhoudende de tyd en de plaats alwaar dit Papier is gevonden geworden.

FINDEREN af dette Papiir ombedes, naar Leilighed gives, at sende
samme til Admiralitets Secretairen i London, eller nærmeste Embedsmand
i Danmark, Norge, eller Sverrig. Tiden og Stædit hvor dette er fundet
ønskes venskabeligt paategnet.

WER diesen Zettel findet, wird hier-durch ersucht denselben an den
Secretair des Admiralitets in London einzusenden, mit gefälliger angabe
an welchen ort und zu welcher zeit er gefundet worden ist.

{175}

THE MYSTERY OF THE magnetic readings is cleared up. The key is disarmingly simple. Adam rapped on the door of my cabin a few minutes ago, carrying in his arms an officer's tunic that was slightly worn and faded, which he presented to me, announcing: "Here is the guilty party."

Immediately I recognized my tunic, which I had left for mending with Andrew, who is in charge of the laundering and upkeep of the officers' clothing – which for several months has been limited to perfunctory repairs – and without letting anything show, I asked if he knew to whom the garment belonged and what reason he had to reproach him.

He replied that Andrew had refused to identify the owner, but that all the same he had confirmed that it was someone who had participated in several expeditions to take magnetic readings. Then he begged me not to punish the guilty party, to which I had no trouble agreeing, especially because, though I did not yet understand how or why, I was beginning to suspect that the guilty party was none other than myself.

"That is all very well," I said. "Now, would you mind explaining why you are bringing this jacket to me?"

"When you dismantled the instruments for taking measurements some days ago, sir, you noted that they were accurate. I thought to myself that there had to be something that was disturbing the instruments, something that was not part of their mechanism but was to be found nearby . . ."

"And you found that piece of a uniform?"

As I uttered those words I seized the garment and studied it more closely, overcome by incredulity. One of its buttons did not shine as brightly as the others; it was the thin iron button with which I had replaced the brass button that I'd thrown into the sea in the cylinder.

I murmured, nearly without noticing: "The iron . . ."

Adam, still standing in front of me, nodded silently. I placed my hand on his shoulder, gave him the jacket, and he went away, treading lightly. As for me, I am more convinced than ever that the slightest thing we do, even with the best intentions, is likely to end in a disaster. Our learned calculations, our meticulous measurements, our precise formulæ – invalidated, all of them, because of me, and a button . . .

Now every time I go out I shall have to be certain that not one person carry on him the smallest bit of iron or the slightest trace of iron filings that could alter our precious instruments, which are renowned for their precision but are nonetheless absolutely easy to deceive.

THEN THIS ASTONISHING thing happened: Franklin, Sir John Franklin, hero of the Arctic, the man who had eaten his boots, died. While more than once Crozier had imagined his own death, depicting it to himself as a gradual and altogether gentle process, warm water progressively covering his mouth, his nose, his ears, his eyes, until it swallowed him entirely and silenced the voices that were disturbing him, never had he imagined that Sir John might depart this life. Sir John, whose refusal to envisage the possibility that their undertaking would fail struck him on certain days as proceeding not so much from an invincible folly as from a kind of courage, as if the Captain had, unlike himself, who took pleasure in facile despair, consciously determined to go on, regardless. Perhaps he really was made of the stuff of heroes. Especially dead.

Sir John's remains were wrapped in the flag of England that he had kept, folded in eight, in his cabin, the very one that his wife had embroidered shortly before his departure. Then, at the height of summer, when the sun had started to melt the ice in spots, creating thin gurgling rivulets and pools of different depths covered treacherously with a soggy layer of snow in which a man, misstepping, could disappear completely, his body was entrusted to the sea. The pack ice did not disappear that summer and the ships remained imprisoned. The ice soon re-formed, crystalline, over Sir John's remains. For months you could see, through a protective coating resembling the glass that isolates precious artifacts from viewers in museums, the colours of the flag that covered the Captain. Exhibited in that way, it seemed to signify unequivocally that it was the ice that had taken possession of Her Majesty's expedition, and not the reverse.

Lady Franklin's Lament

You seamen bold, that have long withstood
Wild storms of Neptune's briny flood.
Attend to these few lines which I now will name,
And put you in mind of a sailor's dream.

As homeward bound one night on the deep,
Slung in my hammock I fell asleep,
I dreamt a dream which I thought was true,
Concerning Franklin and his brave crew.

I thought as we neared to the Humber shore,
I heard a female that did deplore,
She wept aloud and seemed to say,
Alas! my Franklin is long away.

Her mind it seemed in sad distress,
She cried aloud I can take no rest,
Ten thousand pounds I would freely give,
To say on earth that my husband lives.

Cathedra foraminata

WHEN SHE WAS NOT BUSY painting her maps that looked like numerous multicoloured labyrinths, Lady Jane plunged back into the journals of Scoresby, Ross, and Parry, all of whom had tried unsuccessfully to discover the passage that her husband had set out to conquer more than two years earlier.

She annotated these narratives that she had consulted a hundred times, as if this time they would give up a secret she hadn't seen before: sometimes she scrutinized them literally with a magnifying glass in the hope of discovering the blanks between the words, small black islands arranged evenly on a mute sea of white. As for what use it would be to her, seated at her desk in the small sitting room of her London house, should she discover the route that must have been taken by her husband, master and prisoner of his iced-in ship at the other end of the world, the problem, while difficult, did not seem insoluble. She had long since developed the habit of finding out by herself the solutions to complex questions and to passing them on without allowing it to show, by osmosis in a sense, to her particularly receptive husband. He would wake up in the morning, after having had the time to consider something that Lady Jane had almost imperceptibly suggested, and he would cry out, delighted, that he had found it. She did not see why a way of doing things that had long been an integral part of the behaviour of the couple would stop working simply because there was an ocean between them.

She tirelessly reread the first volumes of *Cosmos: A Sketch of the Physical Description of the Universe*, the great work of her dear von Humboldt, which had just appeared in English translation. *Cosmos* offered an admirable description of the physical world, whose universal laws it is possible to infer from its details, just as one can deduce from those same laws the singular manifestations of different observed phenomena. That wonderful symmetry which harmoniously united, in an unceasing exchange, the general and the specific seemed to Lady Jane the quintessence of Science. It proceeded at the same time and in equal measure from Knowledge and Philosophy, from Technology and Literature, and seemed to her moreover to mysteriously confirm her own instincts.

With her practical, scientific mind, Lady Jane had never put much store in fortune tellers, hypnotists, or other charlatans who claimed they could read the future, but here it was a matter of reading the present. The one obstacle then was that of distance, of matter – a problem easily resolved, as witness the experiments of Dr. Mesmer and the more recent ones of Mr. Morse.

Lady Jane wrote to Sir John almost every evening, long letters crammed with details, with shades of opinion, with observations and recommendations. He would not read these missives before he came home but she almost believed that she need only write the words on paper and they would find a way to reach her husband in one form or another – perhaps, who knows, in a dream? Surely such an exchange of distant thoughts would not be all that different from the wonders attributed to magnetism, and if one of the Earth's poles could attract all those magnetized needles, why should her husband's mind not attract the words sent to him by his wife from across the sea?

SIR JOHN FRANKLIN DIED two weeks ago and it is not until today that I dare to write those words that until now I have refused to write, as if one could suspend, erase the fact of his death. He was found lifeless on the morning of June 11, his face at peace, lying on his bunk, dressed in the uniform he had worn the night before. No one knows the cause, and I have forbidden Peddie, who wanted to perform an autopsy, to search through his entrails, which seemed to me an unnecessary insult. Although it would have done no harm to my vanity, while in England, to have been made commander of the expedition, still, it displeases me more than I can say to think that I now owe it to a man's death.

The day after Sir John died, DesVoeux asked me if I wished to move onto the *Erebus,* where apparently Sir John's cabin is more spacious than mine. Naturally I refused, stipulating that nothing must be touched. Fitzjames, who for the most part was already seeing to it that everything on board was in good working order, is now Captain of the *Erebus* and my Second-in-Command. Surprising as it may seem, I discover that I am happy that I can count on him.

I prayed only once on Sir John's grave and could stay for just a few minutes before that odd display case formed by the ice covering the flag that wraps his body. I understand why we take care to bury the dead or to entrust their bodies to the depths of the sea: it is not natural to continue seeing them for so long after their demise, or to feel as if they can go on contemplating us after their eyes are closed forever.

Had it not been so laughable, it would be something to cry over. I invented a rival from whole cloth. Who knows what other tricks my imagination may have played?

Fitzjames, in spite of a genuine talent for drawing – witness the series of officers' portraits executed freehand while the models were busy downing their port, which, when distributed to the men, gave them great pleasure – swears by the daguerreotype and insisted on supervising its loading, as well as that of the hundreds of copper plates carefully stacked in the hold of the *Erebus*.

The device, somewhat cumbersome and inconvenient, requires patience and meticulousness equal to that needed for the declination compasses, but the process necessary to develop the image at the end of the exposure time is so complex and delicate that I sometimes find myself longing for the time when a pen and a scrap of paper were enough to portray any landscape – as they still are to draw any map.

It goes without saying that scientific progress is a wonderful thing and that it allows us to spread further every day our dominion over the world around us, but the sight of Fitzjames with his eyes creased, bent over his basins steaming with mercury and sodium hyposulphite, makes me feel as if I have wandered by accident into the laboratory of some alchemist of bygone days, absorbed in executing his Great Work.

The result of these operations, however, never ceases to amaze me and I cannot accustom myself to this marvel whereby we manage to set down on silver a genuine object, or, more precisely, its image. This is truly a marvel close to sorcery and I have sometimes wondered if a consequence of this process is to strip the depicted object of a fleeting but essential part of itself. When observing the image that is taking shape we feel we are witnessing the appearance of some ghostly form that has lost its substance and is now simply a blank surface. The collection of daguerreotypes produced since the beginning of our voyage seems to me to show something like the underside or the shadow of what we have truly observed.

When I opened my heart to Fitzjames about these reflections just now, as he was busy dismantling the device in order to wipe off any trace of condensation, he laughed heartily.

"Francis, do you think that by executing someone's portrait in oil or charcoal we steal some fragment of his being?"

"No, of course not . . ."

"Basically, the daguerreotype does nothing different, except that for the uncertain hand and eye of the artist it substitutes the unerring accuracy of the mechanism."

I am well aware that he is right, but nonetheless, the notion of those images separated forever from their model, leading apart from him an independent life, bothers and displeases me.

I asked him if he had executed portraits before he embarked on the *Erebus*.

"Yes, a few, during the weeks before our departure, to become familiar with the device. Lady Jane, Sir John's wife, who was curious to learn everything about the mechanism, and also her niece, a rather pretty young person whose name I do not recall."

"Sophia."

And so it is to him that I owe the only image I possess of the woman I think about day and night, he who cannot recall her name.

"Yes, Sophia. I had to redo the plate several times if memory serves. She wouldn't hold still."

I mumbled something or other and staggered out, like a man who is intoxicated, at the thought of Sophia wriggling with pleasure before the camera's cold eye.

— Adam?

— Yes.

— Are you asleep?

— No.

— I'm hungry.

— I know. Go to sleep and you won't feel the hunger.

— What about you?

— Yes.

— Do you think it will go on much longer?

— Longer?

— Being iced in. Do you think the ice will give way soon so the ships can leave?

— I don't know.

— Neither do I, no one knows. But what do you think?

— The truth?

— No.

— I think it's a matter of days. The sun is a little stronger every day. Soon they will start up the engines again and smash all this ice as easily as a person can shatter the ice that covers the ponds in the moors after the last freeze-up in spring. Today I saw cracks that weren't there yesterday. And then the icefields will open by themselves and it will be summer.

— Will there be birds?

— Enough to fill the sky. Thousands. Gulls, terns, fine plump geese with lush red flesh. There will be foxes, too, and herds of reindeer that will come to graze nearby.

— Adam?

– Yes.

– What do you miss most of all?

– The horizon. Knowing where the earth stops and where the sky begins. Not having to picture an imaginary line between the white and the white . . .

– I miss my wife, Adam. Every day I think about her all day long, and I see her in my dreams, but she runs away as soon as I try to come near her. I wish I were lying beside her in a real bed, with an eiderdown, and watching the sun rise through the window while I listen to her breathing at my side.

– . . .

– Adam?

– Yes.

– Now, the truth.

– I don't know.

– The truth, I said.

– We're at the end of July. Since we arrived at more or less the same time last year, it means there was no ice then and there is now. The maps that we have cannot tell us whether this year is particularly cold or last year was particularly mild. In either case, it will soon be autumn and we shall have to wait for another spring before we can leave.

– Adam?

– Yes.

– I'm hungry.

– I know, go to sleep, then you won't feel the hunger.

– She runs away as soon as I try to come near her, Adam.

– I know.

FOR SOME WEEKS NOW Sophia has been unable either to sleep properly or to stay awake, and she spends most of her days slumped on a sofa, victim of a kind of drowsiness, unable to take an interest in anything, unable even to read more than a few pages at a time. At night she sleeps badly, gets up in the morning pale and drawn after struggling for hours in dreams, retaining of them only a vague sense of ill-being and some hazy images. A man introduces himself first as John Fitzjames and then, turning around, reveals behind his skull the face of Mathieu de Longchamp, who is then transformed into Francis Crozier. With a multitude of partners, she dances to a strident-sounding waltz in a ballroom where the crystal and gold give off a brilliance similar to what one sees in a kaleidoscope. The dancers and the flashes of light move to the rhythm of the racing violins, to explode in a highly charged sarabande from which Sophia is excluded. She wakes up in a cold sweat, the pallid light of dawn seeping in through the partly open shutters; not a sound can be heard from either the deserted street or inside the house, where everyone is still asleep. She is alone, trying to control the beating of her heart, which flutters in brief surges. She breathes deeply, picks up a book in which she makes out a few paragraphs in the half-light, rereads them twice, three times without remembering a word, then finally goes back to sleep when the first servants are getting up, to the sound of running water and muffled footsteps on the main floor. Certain images of the night pursue her for days at a time: Crozier's face, oddly transplanted onto the body of another man; his eyes that express a never-ending reproach.

2 September 1847

For over two years we have been in this land of snow and I have more and more trouble remembering my life before: County Down where I spent my childhood, my previous missions, the ships on which I served and the crews in whose company I lived, my last expedition to the Antarctic, the preparations for this voyage, even the few blessed weeks spent in Tasmania seem to me now part of a dream. I often recall snatches of it, generally without wanting to and sometimes at oddly ill-timed moments, but as soon as I try to hang on to them, to evoke images that I know could not have been erased from my memory, they fray and scatter as if I were trying to scoop up armfuls of spindrift. In the same way I am incapable of imagining an "after" to this icy stay that seems to me as bereft of an ending as it is devoid of a beginning. I know, of course, thanks to this journal, thanks to the instruments, that it has been exactly 723 days that we have been prisoners of whiteness, but they could just as well have been a few very long days, or decades. Time is no longer a familiar measure, regular as a metronome, an absolute and absolutely consistent benchmark. The skein of the hours and the days has been unwound, leaving me but one moment, everlasting and forever started afresh.

Life on board a ship held captive of the ice and the night in the far reaches of the known world is virtually unbearable for two paradoxical reasons: it is a life of utter isolation, and utterly lacking in privacy, two conditions that, while opposite, are equally contrary to human nature. Man requires the company of his fellow creatures, on that we agree. But forced to spend every second of every day in the midst of other men, one may come to see them solely as animals who eat, drink, shit, and piss, who fight and sometimes die. This small society, moreover, lives in an isolation so complete that it could just as well be alone in the world. Having come as discoverers to survey an unknown land and to ply some legendary waters, the men see their kingdom reduced to the size of two wooden ships of which they know, after a few weeks, every square inch, every nail, every plank, every spot, and every fissure. That is why most attempt to escape through dreams or memory.

Winter is a fearsome creature that bites, claws, gnaws, and devours its victims, slowly but surely. It splits nails and brings into bloom on ice and glass flowers as delicate as lace, their beauty malevolent; it numbs both limbs and mind and even the soul, which now wishes for nothing but to melt into this silent whole whose murderous purity seems like rest and peace.

To move is pain, to breathe is pain, for it means allowing the creature of frost to enter oneself, to take over one's being and freeze it all the way to the heart.

The breath of the men rises in clouds from their partly

open lips, as if with each exhalation part of their soul escaped, dissolved, and disappeared into the icy air. The frost seeps into the slightest chinks, becomes embedded in imperceptible cracks that it swells until the planks burst, clattering like thunder. A fine white powder covers every surface, resembling the downy moss whose apparent softness conceals a cold as dry as bone. Anyone who inadvertently places a bare finger on a metal object is forced, to free it, to leave behind shreds of flesh.

AS THE MONTHS WENT BY, Lady Jane's anxiety grew. She had confided in some of the gentlemen members of the Royal Geographical Society and the Royal Society, but they had brushed aside her doubts, reminding her that the *Erebus* and the *Terror*, iron-armed giants propelled by powerful engines and carrying more than enough provisions to feed their crews for three years if necessary, must be making short work of the Arctic ice. Perhaps the Passage had long since been discovered and Franklin was now attempting to find a more direct route, or one more easily negotiable by ships less powerful than his. Perhaps he had set out upon a detailed reconnaissance of this region, the maps of which were in large part blank. Jane wrote to the Admiralty, where her missives were given the same treatment and remained unanswered. Obviously no one was willing to consider that the Franklin expedition could be in a sorry plight. On the contrary, everyone needed to believe that its success was ineluctable.

But Lady Jane was not a woman to be discouraged by such a small matter and she did not intend to be politely sent home like the wife of a foot soldier come to ask for word about her husband, whose arm is patted while encouraging words are murmured and who leaves empty-handed.

These gentlemen were on their own turf in the Admiralty headquarters or comfortably settled in easy chairs at their club. They had numbers and the battlefield to themselves; this was obviously unacceptable and a way must be found to gain the advantage.

Lady Jane decided to invite them to share her Christmas dinner.

After much thought, to this dinner which seemed to her to represent, if not her last, then at least her best hope of bringing these gentlemen around to her point of view, she invited:

- Sir John Barrow, first baronet, second secretary of the Admiralty, Fellow of the Royal Society and of the London Geographical Society, and his charming wife;

- James Clark Ross, seasoned explorer, recipient of the Legion of Honour and Fellow of the London Geographical Society, and his charming wife;

- Sir Robert Peel, Prime Minister, and his charming wife (who were known to spend Christmas with her parents in Devonshire, but all the same it would not be disagreeable to announce to the other guests: "Sir Robert, who regrets that he is unable to join us, but as you well know, our first responsibility is to our family, sends greetings . . .");

- William Edward Parry, he too a highly skilled explorer, rear admiral, and governor of the Greenwich Hospital, and his charming wife;

- Jim Foster, fish merchant whose shop was located in Castle Street in the same village as the castle of Sir James Forester, inventor and Fellow of the London Geographical Society, for whom the invitation was intended but who did not receive it. Consequently, he was unable to respond and was never again invited by Lady Jane. As for Jim Foster, after a moment's incredulity, he used the envelope which had held the invitation to wrap a piece of cod and thought no more about it;

↠ Sir Lionel Templar, man of science and also a Fellow of the Royal Geographical Society (whose charming wife had passed away some months before and who was in the habit of spending Christmas with his daughter).

James Ross, William Parry, and John Barrow replied that they would be delighted to spend Christmas in the company of the wife of their colleague and friend, the former specifying that he would be overjoyed to meet the daughter of the latter. Lady Jane was forced to admit that she had completely forgotten Eleanor, having supposed that she would spend Christmas with her fiancé's family. Inexplicably, it took a great deal of persuading before Eleanor accepted her stepmother's invitation, which she promised to honour only on condition that Lady Jane invite her future in-laws, too. After doing her best to deter the young woman (those people will be bored to death, they don't know anyone, our circle being so different from theirs they would only be ill-at-ease, do think about it, Eleanor), Lady Jane gave in and directed her energy elsewhere, refusing to worry any more at the thought that Sir John Barrow would be forced to rub shoulders with those Gells, whose fortune (recent) had to do with cloth or lace, she was not sure which. Sir Robert Peel made it known that he was sorry but that he was engaged elsewhere. He graciously thanked Lady Jane for her invitation and promised to visit her in the new year. As for Sir James Forester, he, needless to say, said not a word, any more than did Lionel Templar, which Lady Jane attributed to bad manners in the case of the first and to the sorrow of bereavement in the second.

The weeks that followed passed quickly in visits, shopping, and various distractions intended to shake Sophia out of the torpor that seemed to have swept over her. The menu was drawn up with the greatest care. Lady Jane hesitated at length between a goose and roast beef, she shilly-shallied over serving an aspic or a sorbet as a palate cleanser, concluding that neither was necessary and that the culinary customs from the other side of the Channel were but a passing fancy. She had long since determined her seating plan, using small place cards decorated by her niece.

It had been particularly cold for some days and when the ladies woke up on Christmas morning they caught sight through their windows of a landscape covered in snow. It was as if the trees had been wrapped in cotton, a spotless blanket thrown onto the grass, the alleys, the streets, even onto the hats of the rare passersby, who were moving quickly for flakes were still falling – lethargic, rounded, like so many balls of fur.

The parlour was decorated simply, as is fitting for a room that is virtually mourning the absence of its most illustrious occupant at a time of year when good taste requires letting oneself be won over by a spirit of merry-making. Tufts of holly had been put up here and there; and garlands of fir adorned with sweet-smelling pomanders surrounded the fireplace and were twisted around the banister, where they resembled vines that were trying to reach upstairs. The flames of dozens of candles were reflected in the crystals of the chandeliers and the gold-framed mirrors, making the room look like a jewel box. Outside, the darkness had a nearly supernatural brilliance; moonbeams bathed in a silvery glow the soft carpet covering the ground.

Sir John and Lady Barrow were first to arrive, soon followed by James and Ann Ross and the Parrys. Eleanor, her fiancé, and the latter's parents kept the others waiting, an unforgivable faux pas in the eyes of Lady Jane, who would have much preferred that they be already seated when her most important guests arrived, to give the impression (since she could not do otherwise) of an amicable family gathering, and that they not monopolize everyone's attention during the long minutes between the moment they were announced and the one when they finally were seated.

Ann Ross, née Coulmann, was scarcely twenty-five years of age, charming but sadly afflicted with such timidity that she had trouble responding to even the most insignificant question and blushed the moment her name was uttered. After the introductions were made she did not open her mouth, joining in the conversation by greeting the repartee of others with a politely astonished smile.

As she had often done during the past months, Sophia asked herself why men married silly, innocent young things incapable, even should their lives depend on it, of sustaining a discussion on any scientific, philosophical, or artistic matter, not even, in one precise case, about the weather. ("This snow is glorious, don't you think?" Sophia had asked. "With all the faded, slightly muffled colours, it is in a way like being in a Turner painting." " . . ." young Mistress Ross had replied, smiling graciously.) Perhaps the gentlemen took pride in the restful silence of their wives. If they were so insistent on having at their sides a gentle, peaceful, and obedient companion, why for heaven's sake did they not instead adopt a female greyhound? Somewhat surprised herself at the violence of the feeling stirred in her by the young person with pink cheeks and vacant eyes, Sophia resolved to be especially kind to Mrs. Ross.

Eleanor, her fiancé, Philip, and his parents arrived just then. Lady Jane hoped that they would at least have the decency to try not to be noticed, but Mrs. Gell, after effusively greeting the ladies present as if they were old acquaintances, launched into a rambling conversation with young Mrs. Ross, whose smile appeared after a while to be a little weary.

While Lady Jane was talking with William Parry about the configuration of a possible Polar sea, Hector, the butler, came to inform her that Sir Lionel Templar had arrived. Without evincing any surprise, Lady Jane greeted the news with a delighted smile, as if she were expecting the arrival of this unexpected guest who had not thought it necessary to reply to her invitation.

Calling Hector back, she instructed him in a low voice to set another place at the table between Eleanor and Philip's father. She would at least punish such rudeness by seating him between two deadly dull table mates.

Hector did not obey immediately, which was unusual.

"I say," said Lady Jane impatiently, "what are you waiting for?"

"Yes, Madam, only . . ."

"Only what, Hector?"

He hesitated, afraid of seeming impertinent.

"Only, Madam, that will make thirteen at table."

Now that was unfortunate.

"Add two settings, then. And move Sir John Barrow so that he is next to Mrs. Parry. The place at the head of the table will be left vacant."

It came time to move into the dining room, which was also decorated with fir boughs and gilt garlands. The long walnut table was covered with an embroidered cloth on which were arranged the Franklin family's finest silver, crystal, and the Wedgwood china that was kept for grand occasions. The guests took their places and Lady Jane announced, pointing to the empty chair at the end of the table, beneath the nearly life-sized portrait of Sir John: "My dear husband and those who are with him are here in our thoughts. This empty chair reminds us of the emptiness that their departure has left in our hearts."

The ladies heaved a tender sigh of sympathy and the gentlemen responded with a virile nod of their heads.

Christmas 1847

MENU

Oysters on the half shell
Oxtail consommé

Stuffed carp

Guinea fowl with black trumpet mushrooms
Casserole of veal sweetbreads in cream sauce

Roasted turkey with chestnut stuffing, cranberry sauce
Potatoes *maître d'hôtel*
Green peas, *à la française*

Cheese
Salade parisienne

Fruit
Biscuits
Meringues

Plum Pudding

IT TURNED OUT THAT young Mistress Ross did not eat meat, as her husband explained on her behalf while the servants were placing in the middle of the table tiered silver platters with raw oysters in their mother-of-pearl shells arranged in a star shape on crushed ice, surrounded by wedges of lemon.

"But my dear," Lady Jane told him, as if she had thought that he'd spoken in jest, "as far as I know oysters are not meat. Your charming wife can enjoy them without fear."

"It's just," the younger woman began, in a voice so low that Lady Jane had to read her lips, "I do not eat fish, either."

"What is this?" cried out Lady Barrow as she noted that something seemed to be impeding the service. Like her husband, she was afflicted with a rather serious hearing problem.

"Mrs. Ross does not eat fish," Mr. Gell informed her obligingly.

"I beg your pardon?" she replied.

"MRS. ROSS DOES NOT EAT FISH," he repeated, so loudly that Eleanor, who was sitting beside him and had missed the beginning of the conversation, was startled and looked at him as if she feared that he had lost his mind.

"But the oyster is not a fish," Sir John Barrow broke in. Having understood, he was happy to contribute this taxonomic correction.

"Ann does not eat crustaceans, either," Ross began, then, seeing that Sir John was threatening to intervene anew: "Or molluscs. Or, indeed, eggs or cheese. Nothing that is animal or that comes from an animal," he concluded, while his silent spouse, her gaze lowered, turned pink before their very eyes.

"Wool, for instance," Sophia murmured between her teeth. Parry, sitting on her right, convinced himself he had heard incorrectly.

Lady Jane, who had very little patience for this kind of caprice, took hold of the closest platter and, exchanging a look of complicity with her niece, extended it to the young woman, smiling:

"Very well, my dear, will you take a slice of lemon?"

Her dear refused politely, but agreed to taste the cranberry sauce, after which she accepted a tiny helping of potatoes and a few peas which Sophia, sitting nearby, estimated to number twelve, before reluctantly eating half an orange from which she removed the sections one at a time with her long, pale fingers while the other guests were at the cheese – Cheddar, Brie, Morbier – and port. (As for Mrs. Ross, she drank only water, even though Lady Jane had assured her that all the grapes in the various wines came exclusively from plants.)

The plum pudding had, as is required, spent the past three weeks wrapped in a cloth, hanging in a cool, airy part of the kitchen where the cook came every day to stir it and lace it with a drop of brandy. To the batter had been added the traditional ring, coin, and thimble (the first ensuring to whoever bit into it a marriage during the year to come; the second, prosperity; and the third, a year of celibacy – but a happy one). The heavy, spongy, spicy lump had then been plunged into some gelatinous beef bouillon where it boiled for four hours, then it was suspended again for one week, after which it was baked for six hours.

The guests expressed polite admiration when the pudding was brought from the kitchen already alight, the ball of fire giving off the fragrance of vanilla, clove, and orange joined by something discreet but heady, like a memory of the odour of suet.

The carafes of Sauternes appeared on the table along with the spectacular dessert Lady Jane insisted on serving herself. Gesturing refusal, Mrs. Ross took a prune and began carefully to peel it. No sooner had the pudding been cut into than Mrs. Gell let out a little cry and, bringing her fingers to her mouth, produced the coin, which she had just bitten. Everyone congratulated her on her good luck and she turned red as if she were being complimented on some exceptional skill or talent that she could be proud of.

Soon Sophia felt between her teeth a hard object that she dreaded. It was nothing, really: she just had to hold up the thimble, smile, and wait for the gibes, most assuredly not too alarming, to be over. But she simply lacked the courage. Unthinking, she used her tongue to push the piece of metal deep into her throat and swallowed it, along with a raisin.

The conversation, rather desultory, carried on; Ross touched upon the famine that continued to devastate Ireland; Lady Jane tried (in vain) to interest Mrs. Parry in a peculiar novel published some months before, the work of an unknown young writer named Ellis Bell; and the gentlemen rejoiced over Kent's victory at croquet, to which they drank a delighted toast.

Just then Eleanor let out a muffled exclamation and took from her mouth the thimble, giving rise to a variety of amused remarks:

"I say, my boy, is your sweetheart having second thoughts?" exclaimed her fiancé's father, laughing.

"I beg your pardon?" said Sir John Barrow, but this time no one replied.

Stoically, Sophia smiled, wondering if the ring, swallowed inadvertently, still had its power as a marriage-maker.

When what was left of the plum pudding, a tepid, slimy, brownish heap, had been taken to the kitchen, when the crystal decanters for the service of Cognac and Glenlivet had been set out, at the moment when the ladies were about to withdraw to let their husbands smoke their cigars in peace, Lady Jane moved in to attack:

"I want to reiterate to all of you that your presence here today is priceless. I thank you for coming to brighten with your company the very sad Christmas of a worried wife . . ." she began, her voice quavering, which brought a stunned look from Eleanor, who was not accustomed to hearing her stepmother speak so tearfully.

" . . . for as you are well aware, my dear John has been gone for nearly three years now and we have not yet received a single word from his expedition. I feel a pang of emotion when I think that he may be in a difficult situation, waiting impatiently perhaps for help to come that we do not even think of sending him . . ."

Parry broke in with the steady voice one uses to persuade a disturbed individual to come down from the roof where he is perched, or to convince him that he is not the object of some plot hatched by foreign powers:

"Dear Jane, do not forget that you are speaking about an expedition that has unprecedented resources. While there have been cases of ships imprisoned in the Arctic ice, they were not as well armed for confronting harsh conditions as the *Erebus* and the *Terror*. And remember, Sir John has valuable experience of a Polar land and he will be best able to decide on the correct procedure for completing his mission with no danger to himself or to his men. Sir John Barrow," he added, raising his glass to the old man, who, cupping his hand to his ear, was trying to grasp what was being said about him, "has seen to it that they are prepared for any eventuality."

"Quite so, quite so," Ross went him one better. "Never has an expedition been so generously equipped, so effectively fitted out. While your fears are entirely normal on the part of a loving wife, you may rest assured that they are groundless."

Sir John Barrow had raised his glass, apparently thinking that he was expected to propose a toast; seeing that no one was following him, he set it down again, and soon his head was nodding gently. Lady Jane, who expected more on the part of the man who had made all the decisions of the Admiralty for nearly forty years, took advantage of the opportunity to regain control of the situation.

"Nonetheless, it seems to me most well advised to launch straightaway one or more rescue expeditions, which in all probability will never be necessary, but should the need arise, would be ready to leave in the spring." She looked down, her voice became a murmur, and when she spoke again she gazed fixedly at the place left empty at the head of the table. "Knowing that the man one loves is so far away, sensing that he is calling out to us, calling for our help when we are unable to do anything, is terrible. Only a sailor's wife can understand the feeling that haunts the heart, the mysterious communication one maintains, in spite of distance, with the man who has gone to sea . . ."

As she had hoped, at those words young Mrs. Ross burst out sobbing. She who had made her fiancé swear that never again would he agree to command so perilous an expedition – when it was suggested that he lead the very one which had eventually been given to Franklin – she saw herself alone, worried, tormented, unhappy, and she could not hold back her imagined sorrow.

"Oh!" she exclaimed, and for the first time Sophia could hear the tone of her voice, which, she had to acknowledge, was not unpleasant. "James, you must do something!"

Lady Jane settled comfortably into her chair.

1 January 1848

SAD, SAD NEW YEAR'S celebration on board the *Terror* to mark the coming of the year 1848. Everyone around the table did his best to look happy, but the faces were grim. Repeated toasts were proposed – to the year that was ending, the one that was coming, to the discovery that we shall not fail to make, to the England we have left in order to extend her dominion beyond the seas, and of which it seems to me that we now dream as others before us have dreamed of Eldorado or the land of milk and honey. I know as I look at the forced smiles on Fitzjames, Little, and Gore that they share my discomfort, that even the stewards who go about their tasks like nervous and awkward automatons can sense it. Perhaps they have forgotten how to serve a festive meal.

With great ceremony the last jars of rillettes and goose pâté were opened, but those tidbits tasted like ashes in my mouth and I had to force myself to swallow them, as if they were some bitter medicine. Those delicacies were too reminiscent of the last meal of a condemned man for anyone in the officers' mess to savour them with pleasure.

I could not resolve to launch into a long-winded speech of the sort that Sir John would gladly make on grand occasions, feeling neither the courage nor the cowardice necessary for lying to these men whose existence I have been sharing for close to three years. At midnight, I contented myself with raising my glass and drinking to their health.

Whatever happens, our last year in the Arctic came to an end last night. Every man knows without it being said that we no longer have rations enough to allow us to survive for one more year amid the ice that does not loosen its embrace.

ALONE IN THE LIBRARY of the *Terror,* where he liked to take refuge when he needed to think, Crozier was pacing, his strides long and nervous, and arrived at nothing save to turn over in his mind the only two choices, each with an equally uncertain outcome: to give up the relative safety of the ships and set out on foot, in the cold and snow, on an expedition of some thousands of miles (and if that were the decision, he would have to determine the best direction to go, which posed a new dilemma) or to risk remaining a prisoner of the two ships that might not be able to escape from the ice in summer (and even if they did, the provisions would be cruelly rationed and there was no guarantee that they could stretch them out so that they would last for the entire trip back to England). As the room was tiny, it took but three steps to cross it, and Crozier stalked angrily back and forth.

He stopped and stood for a moment with his arms dangling, then he emptied a whole carton of books without knowing what he might hope to find in it. When he was a child his grandmother had been in the habit of every morning opening the Bible at random, putting her finger blindly on a page, and reading aloud the verse to which she had pointed, swearing that this teaching would be valuable to her for the day to come. Filled with wonder at this unexpected opportunity to draw from the divine source some nearly supernatural wisdom, the young Francis had sometimes tried to imitate her, but he had obtained only cryptic, even incomprehensible results – unless they were dull and trivial.

"*After he brought me through the entry, which was at the side* of the gate, into the holy chambers of the priests, which looked towards the north."

"Thou crownest the year with thy goodness; and thy paths drop fatness."

"And it shall come to pass after these events."

He had soon turned his attention to the few science books that his uncle, who was very keen on geography and mushrooms, possessed, books with pictures.

In the half-light in the belly of the *Terror*, where floated an aroma of coal, dampness, and mouldy paper, Crozier picked up the volumes one by one, arranged them absent-mindedly around him in a fan. *The Vicar of Wakefield*, which had always seemed to him to be intended for the weaker sex. Shakespeare. The *Sonnets*, *Othello*, *King Lear*. Newton. A collection of French poems. A work of botany. A heavy etymological dictionary bound in brown leather which fell, open, as Crozier was placing it on an unsteady pile. Picking it up again, his eyes fell on the entry for *tea*.

First tay *(1652), then* tea *(1657) according to modern Latin; derived from Malayan* teh, te, *or from the word* t'e *in southern Chinese dialects by way of the Dutch language. The plant is originally from Asia and both botany and Chinese medicine trace it back to the third millennium B.C., during the reign of Shennong, a mythical emperor. Identified by various Chinese names, it was reputed to relieve fatigue, strengthen the will, and sharpen the eyesight. In the 5th or 4th century B.C., it spread into the valley of the Yangtze and into southern China, and it then began to be identified by the current ideogram* 茶 *which is transcribed as* cha, *no doubt derived from the classical character* tu. *In the west the word turns up several times (in 851 in Arabic, by the merchant Soliman) before the plant was imported into Europe in 1606 by the Dutch East India Company, which had been founded four years earlier. Several languages have borrowed from classical Chinese* cha, *the name by which they identify tea, among them Portuguese* (cha), *Russian* (tchai), *Turkish, and Persian. The multiplicity of commercial routes explains why we cannot decide between the Chinese and the Malayan etymon.*

He reread the last sentences, incredulous, then burst out laughing. He felt tears coming to his eyes, running down his cheeks, wetting his whole face with their bitter water. This business of the *T* drawn on the crates was nonsense, as he had been well aware . . . And now it was too late.

In a kind of frenzy, he grabbed the books he had arranged around him and began to skim them methodically, with suppressed rage, turning the pages of entire chapters at a time, shaking the volumes as if to make them give up he didn't know what, even striking the spine on the ground when the volume had not released any secret following his violent examination.

Then they sat there, books and commander, shaggy-haired, bruised, desperately mute.

THE HEAVY CRIMSON velvet curtains had been drawn and the small sitting room was filled with a half-light similar to the kind that bathes the naves of churches. Lighted candles in every corner cast misshapen shadows on walls covered with flowered paper. The ladies, who numbered eight, of whom Lady Jane and Sophia knew only the lady of the house and her sister, were speaking in hushed voices and letting out small laughs which they quickly stifled, like excited schoolgirls before the prizes are handed out. A round table in the middle of the room, covered for the occasion with a dark cloth that fell to the floor in thick folds, was surrounded by eleven straight-backed chairs.

Without introducing them to her other guests, Mrs. Parry gestured to Lady Jane and Sophia to take a seat. They sat side by side, soon copied by the other women, whose age ranged from around twenty (a long, pale, blond girl) to late fifties (a white-haired matron with a heavy bosom). The table fell silent when Mrs. Parry fetched in Miss Ellen Dawson, a medium by trade. Short and plump, she moved with grace and had a pleasantly round face on which one could not however make out the features, hidden as they were by a small black veil that formed a mask to the chin, an accessory that helped her, so she said, to disregard what was around her, the better to concentrate on the message that would come from the beyond. She had an accent impossible to identify, which combined the musicality of some mysterious Slavic language with some nasal vowels of purest Cockney.

"Take the hands of your neighbours," she said, with a slight rolling of the *r*, "and close your eyes."

Nine pairs of eyelids were lowered straightaway. Miss Dawson studied attentively each of the ladies seated around the table, when her turn came looking deeply into the eyes of Lady Jane, who was observing her, too.

"Very well, I believe this lady has a question for me," she said, indicating Lady Jane, who remained silent.

If this Miss Dawson was able to hear the voices of those who had passed on and to interpret the speech of the dead for the benefit of the living, then it stood to reason that she must be able to hear the question that was haunting Lady Jane, seated across from her, without her having to state it aloud.

"I have a question," interrupted – most impolitely, thought Lady Jane and Sophia, who both pursed their lips – a small lady with red hair. "I should like to know if Josephine is happy where she is now. Please, Miss Dawson . . ."

Miss Dawson released the hand of the woman on either side of her and raised her arms, at the same time throwing her head back. Her body stiffened, then she dropped her arms and announced in a changed voice: "Yes, she is at peace . . . She has a message for you: she forgives you. She has long since forgiven you." At these words, the red-haired lady could not repress a sob. She directed an expressive look at her neighbour, who apparently knew who Josephine was and why there was need of forgiveness, for she murmured: "That is extraordinary . . ."

Miss Dawson studied the neighbour for a moment, then returned her gaze to Lady Jane: "It's not a dead man whom you wish to know about. The one to whom you want to speak is alive, in a land of cold and darkness."

"Is he safe and well?" Lady Franklin could not prevent

herself from crying out.

"I cannot say. The images that come to me are blurred. I see water, stones. I see a powerful man and a flag. Everything is white, hazy . . ."

Her voice faded and she turned towards Sophia, sitting on the edge of her chair with bated breath: "You have already had the answer to your question but you refused to hear it."

Miss Dawson relaxed all at once and rested her head on her arms. Mrs. Parry almost had to carry her out of the room. The ladies rose, shaken and for the most part disappointed for they had not had time to question their own dead. The curtains were thrown open and a tentative daylight came in, shedding light on pale faces. What had started as an innocent entertainment, a curiosity, had been transformed into a disturbing and rather trying exercise. Lady Jane rushed out, leaving her shawl on the back of her chair. When Sophia came back to fetch it, Miss Dawson signalled to her, beckoning her into the small room where she was sitting before a platter covered with cheeses and pâtés. She chewed for several seconds, swallowed, then stated almost absent-mindedly: "Place a mirror under your pillow every night and on the fourteenth day you will see in it the man who will be your husband," after which she took a long gulp of wine and settled into her chair.

In the small parlour, the red-haired lady was still sniffling: "It is such a relief to know that Josephine is happy. When the coach ran over her last month I thought that I would never forgive myself. But she adored putting herself in the horses' way and trying to bite their legs . . ." Her voice broke and her friend put her arm around the woman's shoulders to comfort her.

The mirror under her pillow formed a hard lump that kept her awake. She had first tried to wrap it in a cashmere scarf but the lump, while not so hard, was bulkier and Sophia was still unable to sleep. Unwrapping the object, she had slid it imperceptibly to the side until its presence no longer disturbed her. She had wakened the next morning to discover that the looking-glass was no longer under her pillow but under the one beside hers – which doubtless resulted in the invalidation of the two previous nights of torture. She had to start again from square one.

Over the nights that followed, she did her best simply to ignore the thing, finally falling asleep, exhausted, at the first light of dawn. Then she moved the mirror so that it took up as little space as possible under the sensitive nape of her neck, but discovered that doing so uncovered the mirror, in which she caught sight when she wakened in the middle of the night of a vague form that she believed to be a ghost before she realized that it was her own silhouette, and turned furiously to the wall. She then tried to find a smaller, less cumbersome looking-glass in her dressing table, turning the contents of its drawers into a tangled mess – a waste of time, save for her discovery of a hatpin adorned with a silver dragonfly, long since presumed lost.

Finally, trying to outsmart it, she placed the mirror under her pillow but slept with her head on the pillow beside it, a stratagem she regretted the next morning, fearing that it obliged her to start again and count the days from zero.

After a few weeks of this intermittent regime, an exasper-ated Sophia resolved to rid herself of the object once and for all and to chase from her mind Miss Dawson and her visions. Her bedroom was sunk in a bluish half-light, the household was asleep, silent. She grabbed the silver handle of the mirror jutting out from under her pillow and stood up, holding it at arm's length as if it were some dangerous animal. In her attempt to place it on her dressing table, she knocked over a candelabrum which took along in its fall a hairbrush and an ebony box holding seashells and pebbles picked up during her travels. It all came crashing to the floor with the sound of breaking glass. Sophia bent over the damage and saw among the conches and agates shining feebly in the moonlight a hundred silver splinters, each reflecting a fragment of everything around it so that she could recognize the individual flowers on the paper that hung on her bedroom walls, the curved leg of the dressing table, the branches of the candelabrum, the moon cut into four by the squares of the casement, and a patch of sky dotted with stars. Carefully, she picked up that last shard. It cut her finger, but she paid no attention, and fell asleep at last holding the splinter of mirror tight in her fist while a drop of blood stained her pillowcase.

THE QUESTION WAS at the centre of every conversation, between the youngest sailor and his neighbour in the next hammock as well as at the Captain's table, where bottles of wine were now opened at dinner only on Saturday: when and how would they get out of the ice? No one dared to broach the underlying question, the real object of everyone's concern, which Crozier himself formulated aloud for the first time on 9 February 1848: would they ever escape from the ice? After a year and a half, a hopeless spring and winter during which the white trap that had closed around the *Terror* and the *Erebus* had not loosened its grip, they must, he said calmly to Fitzjames, who was calculating their position for the thousandth time — for the ships were moving eastward, imperceptibly, carried along by ice that was subject to mysterious currents — they must consider the possibility that the icefield in the sea off King William's Land might never give way. Fitzjames looked up and responded almost mechanically, as if he had had the opportunity to repeat on numerous occasions the remark he made: "Crozier, if we have arrived here by sailing, common sense says that we can leave by the same means."

"I do not believe that the Arctic ice is as concerned about common sense as we are, James. And what if this bay had been free of ice in the summer of 1846 for the first time in a thousand years? And if it took another thousand years before open water were found there?"

"Is that your opinion? That things happen here once every thousand years rather than repeating themselves again and again for all eternity?"

There was something comforting in the words *for all eternity*, a nearly religious, calming quality. Crozier sighed. Now that he had expressed aloud the fear that each of them nourished in secret, he knew that he could no longer ignore it and that he must act.

"I believe the time has come to study the various choices available to us," he said.

"An excellent idea. I was unaware that we had choices," retorted Fitzjames curtly. He busied himself for a few moments adjusting his sextant, which had no need of it, then spoke again, his tone less abrupt. "Very well, Francis, if you believe we are at that point, let us ask the question of the officers, you can hear the opinion of each and then do as you please – as you've always done."

Crozier smiled faintly and felt himself nearly falter. It seemed to him that a terrible burden had just fallen onto his shoulders which he now must carry until death.

YESTERDAY I BROUGHT together the officers of both ships in the mess of the *Terror* and presented the situation they've been fearing for weeks, ever since bread has no longer been baked and even the sea biscuits crawling with maggots have become a rare luxury.

The faces around me were grave. Hollow cheeks, bright eyes, trembling hands: the young officers seemed to be living in the bodies of old men.

"We cannot remain here any longer," I said simply. "As most of you already know, we do not have enough coal to hold out for another winter, or even another autumn, and we have rations left for a few months at most. We must leave the ships and set out on foot."

My words were met by silence. All eyes were on me, but I do not know if the majority saw me. Then DesVoeux asked in a peculiarly shrill voice: "Where are we supposed to go in the middle of this blasted continent of snow?"

I reminded him that twenty years ago Parry and I had left abundant provisions in Prince Regent Inlet, where we had buried in caches nearly everything from the *Fury,* which was too badly damaged to go back to sea. From there it would no doubt be possible to head back up north to Lancaster Sound, where ships are relatively numerous. I felt an imperceptible easing among the men.

DesVoeux snickered and asked if I had heard the rumours

shortly before our departure claiming that those caches had been plundered, or were about to be, by some unscrupulous whalers. These tales had reached me, of course, as had others: that not far away there was an Esquimaux city of ice palaces shining in the sun; that in these waters were whales with the gift of speech; and that there were islands where the birds sang hymns in Latin. Stories by sailors with too much time on their hands, as I tried to explain to him, but already his restlessness had come back and was affecting the others, each of whom began to express his opinions aloud, determined to make himself heard amid a growing cacophony.

I demanded silence. All obeyed, looking at me. Once again I yielded the floor to DesVoeux: "What if we made our way instead towards the west? The mouth of Great Fish River is no farther than the cache where the provisions are hidden, and unlike it, we know that we will find the river intact where it has always been."

Some nervous laughs greeted his last remark. But he was right. The route to the mouth of the river was no longer than the one that led to Prince Regent Inlet. The river, however, was still cruelly distant from our goal, as Fitzjames emphasized:

"And you suggest that we drag the *Terror* or the *Erebus* and then sail the seven hundred miles to Fort Resolution or Fort Providence?"

DesVoeux shrugged:

"Of course not. We need only bring perhaps eight rowing boats that we shall use as well for transporting the provisions and the gear necessary for the expedition. Is that not the practice of those Esquimaux whose virtues and ingenuity you praise so enthusiastically?"

"Indeed," I broke in, "except that they do not drag wooden boats heavier than they are, and if you recall, it is not they who are harnessed but their dogs."

Little, who until then had been silent, asked why we would not try to enlist the services of those Esquimaux who, without a doubt, know better than we do the territory we shall have to cross, and whose dogs and sledges could be of great use to us. Moreover, he added, so long as we supply the necessary weapons, they could no doubt shoot down some game only they know about, so that the remaining provisions would last longer. I reminded him that it was the custom of the Esquimaux to move about in small groups and that it would be surprising if four or five of them, even fitted out with rifles, could feed a crew of more than one hundred men.

Once again, DesVoeux shrugged and made no reply. Most of the men were looking down to avoid meeting my gaze. Coming back to the question of whether it was better to start walking towards the west or towards the east, Fitzjames conceded that the territory around the mouth of the Great Fish River was known to abound with game and provided a habitat for a great many horned animals and vast numbers of birds, while the coast near to Prince Regent Inlet was likely to be desolate and deserted, as I admitted myself, but this only made the difficult decision even harder. I remembered the children's game in which one asks as seriously as possible whether someone would rather lose an arm or a leg, and it seems to me that today we were asking for a response to a similar question. But this time, once the reply is given, I shall not go off to hunt pigeons with other young rascals like me; rather, a blade will indeed fall, but I am not able to say on whom or on what.

My life is no longer terribly important, but upon me a hundred other lives depend. I find myself missing Sir John in a cowardly way, not that I think he would be able to make a more enlightened decision, but because he would relieve me of a weight from which I cannot free myself.

27 February 1848

It is now almost as cold on the boats as on the icefield, the wooden flanks of the ships offering most imperfect protection from the wind that blows here over hundreds of miles without encountering any obstacles and forces its way into the most minuscule cracks, producing a lugubrious hissing that sounds like the breath of a dying creature. The boilers are now operated only two hours a day, and we muster the men below decks where the temperature goes up a few degrees; just as in England, stables and pigsties stay warm thanks to the animals packed into them. The men spend the entire day muffled in layers and layers of wool; one sees virtually no sign of their uniforms under the scarves, gloves, and headgear. At meal times in the officers' mess this creates strange sights that might come straight from a dream, when the silhouettes covered in wool and leather, gesturing awkwardly, their gait hampered by the thickness of the garments, conscientiously carry silver trays holding a brownish, foul-smelling gruel that last year even Neptune would have rejected. One could think them the crew of some ghost ship.

Peddie and MacDonald can do little for the chapped skin, chilblains, and other injuries caused by the cold for which there exist, alas, very few remedies. Everything is done to limit exposure to the elements, crew members are advised to rub their hands, their feet, even their faces regularly, but several are all too happy for the pain in their extremities to stop and would rather lose some toes than feel that pain return.

Tonight I decided that I would order an additional ration of rum to be distributed after supper, then thought better of it and instead asked Peddie to bring out a few volumes of the monumental herbarium on which he has been working almost since our departure. The men avidly shared the notebooks and plunged into them with happy abandon as if they were setting off for a stroll through the fields. Touching cautiously with numb fingers the delicate outlines of the flowers fixed to the paper, it was almost as if they had miraculously discovered a fragment of summer in the middle of this winter that has swept through everywhere.

28 February 1848

I left the *Terror* by myself this afternoon and set out westward, where the mythic Passage is supposed to be found which I fear we shall never cross alive. A few men were outside, drawing water from holes made in the ice. They hailed me and I did not reply. I walked for hours under the white sun, obeying the strange determination that had taken hold of me. The snow on the icefield formed breakers and swells similar to those on a choppy sea, the difference being that on earth they are of a mineral fixedness, like a daguerreotype of liquid waves, a copy deprived of movement that looks dead. There was no sound but the wind on the plain and the creaking of my boots on the hard snow.

A few hours later, I caught sight of tracks left by the Esquimaux, who we had thought had disappeared into some other territory, for it has been more than two months since they stopped visiting us. They are staying nearby, then, but invisible. At that moment I imagined that these inhabitants of Polar lands and a French gentleman by the name of Bergerac, who writes novels, possess a knowledge unknown to us, that would allow us, should we master it, to escape by the air, thanks to the condensation of all the water around us that soaks us to the very core, or through the grace of some mechanical wonder. For one brief moment I fancied the *Terror* and the *Erebus* opening out their immense masts and starting to beat their wings so as to rise peacefully above the water like two great lazy birds. Looking up, I thought I noticed some indistinct spots in the cloudless sky, which always stayed in the periphery of my gaze and vanished as soon as I tried to look directly at them. There is nothing unusual about the phenomenon; it can be attributed, like so much else, to the snow blindness that strikes exhausted eyes with daylight reflected off the white of the ice.

The sun dropped until it touched the Earth and the sky was briefly filled with the colours of the rainbow. The huge ball of fire tipped over the horizon in red and orange folds, while higher up, clouds fringed with gilt were coloured with purple, blue, green. I was strangely moved at this sight which I felt I was witnessing almost as a voyeur, perhaps because I was alone to contemplate it.

The day star disappeared and I turned to go home. To tell the truth I do not know what I was going to look for during this long walk, and I could not say whether I thought I had found it or had resigned myself to not discovering it, but I came back filled with a feeling of peace that has perhaps more to do with fate. No doubt the man who has nothing left to lose and knows it is infinitely freer than one who fears that at any moment he will see his happiness, his wealth, his life get away from him.

CURIOUSLY, SOPHIA, who had always adored balls – to the point of having herself driven one evening to the Gramecys', who were holding a party for which the preparations had been in the headlines for weeks, though she was running a fever and had trouble even standing up – was not, when she thought about Mrs. Rimple's annual do, filled with her usual happy sense of expectation.

While these parties had always struck her as the last word where entertainment was concerned, she had caught herself the week before *yawning* right in the middle of the Carletons' ballroom, where, champagne glass in hand, she was listening to a young captain who, while he had never laid eyes upon a battlefield, had nonetheless an impressive collection of war stories to tell, which had in common their way of highlighting the courage he would soon surely have the opportunity to put to the test against the enemy. Who that enemy was, Sophia was uncertain, and she had not felt a need to question the young man, who pursued his narrative imperturbably. His story was certainly not one of the most fascinating, and normally she would have paid no attention to it, simply let herself be lulled by the music and the murmur of conversations while she gazed at the spectacle of the gowns and the hairstyles, the dancing couples who came together and moved apart beneath the crystals and the gilding that lent their brilliance to these enchanted evenings. And yet she had yawned. It was true that for some months she had experienced problems sleeping but all the same this was phenomenal. Was it possible that she no longer experienced the same pleasure in the company of brilliant young men, elegantly attired, with exquisite manners? Was she ill?

When Lady Jane and Sophia arrived at Mrs. Rimple's most of the guests had been there for some time already. Wisps of hair escaped from the coiffures of young girls rosy-cheeked from excitement. Middle-aged ladies were fanning themselves energetically while the gentlemen, young and old alike, strolled among the crinolines, distributing rapt gazes here and there. From the top of the staircase that looked down on the ballroom, Sophia had in a flash a vision of a cackling barnyard. She swallowed a nervous laugh.

Lady Jane was quickly caught up by acquaintances who wanted to know all they could about the Polar expedition, about Sir John's discoveries, and the probable date of his return; as was her habit, she did her best to be the worthy spokeswoman for her heroic spouse. Sophia moved away, passed absent-mindedly through the crush, and emerged in a room of more modest size and not so crowded, where small groups were conversing. There, she found Amelia next to an attractive pianoforte, busy resisting the entreaties of a young man who, if one were to believe him, had come to Mrs. Rimple's solely for the pleasure of hearing her voice. Taking Sophia as witness that it had been *centuries* since she had touched the instrument, she sat on the bench and let her fingers run across the ivory and ebony keyboard. There rose up an odd music that was at once fluid and disjointed, in which one could first distinguish each solo note in isolation, then perceive the group of which it was a part, where two voices seemed at once to respond to and to shy away from one another. Sophia came to a halt to listen more comfortably to this strange melody that she seemed to be hearing for the first time.

While the first bars were being developed Sophia, fascinated, grasped instinctively that the two melodic lines forming the counterpoint were not answering one another but, similar and distinct, paid each other no attention, and that it was at the heart of this insurmountable, never-filled distance that the clear mystery of Bach's music was to be found. The two melodies were unfurling, isolated, straight, and parallel, their destiny never to meet but for each to reveal the other through their differences, their discrepancies, and their furtive resonances.

Das Wohltemperierte Klavier

Praeludium 1

She sensed the presence of Mathieu de Longchamp without turning around. He suggested a stroll in the garden and she agreed as though it were the most natural thing in the world. They walked onto the terrace, went down a few steps, and slowly turned onto a path covered with small pebbles that crunched under their feet.

"No doubt you will be surprised," said Mathieu, "to learn that I wrote to you on numerous occasions when you were in Tasmania and I never received a reply."

As she said nothing he went on in a tone that was meant to be ironic:

"I came to believe that the ships carrying my letters had all been mysteriously wrecked before they reached their destination, or that there were in Hobart two ladies named Sophia Cracroft and that my missives were being delivered to the wrong one, who, reading them but not understanding a word, considered it quite unnecessary to reply . . ."

She remained silent, waiting for what would come next. His smile was acerbic but it did not ruin his features; on the contrary it lent them a certain firmness that ordinarily was lacking: "Either you gave in to the charms of a particularly seductive prisoner and devoted yourself night and day to working out a plan for escape, which obviously left you no time to answer my letters . . . Or to the attractions of a valiant captain, for 'tis said that you received a good many visitors during your exile, important ones, at that . . ."

She broke in, placing her hand on his arm: "I should have answered your letters, Mathieu, I'm sorry that I did not. But all is for the best, is that not true? In any case, here you are happily betrothed . . . Or are you now married?"

"Not yet. My fiancée and I have decided to wait for the restoration of the manor to be finished and hold the ceremony there. But that changes nothing, of course: rest assured that my happiness knows no bounds."

"I do not doubt that."

"I hope so."

Now his smile was not so harsh, and he suggested to Sophia that she seat herself on a stone bench not far from a gurgling fountain, at the foot of a tremendous statue depicting a half-naked faun.

"I noticed you at the party given by Lady Cornell in honour of her daughter's betrothal . . ."

"You mean of your betrothal . . ."

"As you wish, of my betrothal, of our betrothal . . . Whatever the case, you were ravishing."

"Thank you for the compliment, which has been deferred for nearly two years. You are too kind."

"I should have liked to pay it in person but I feared I would be unable to hold back and I'd have asked you to run away with me . . ."

She looked at him, dumbfounded, wondering if he was serious or had simply wanted to push their flirtation a little further. Deciding that it was best to ignore his last remark, she looked up into the sky scattered with stars, seeking without realizing it the *S* that Francis Crozier had drawn there for her some seven years earlier. She did not find the constellation created specially for her but she envisaged four bright stars crossed through perpendicularly by a line formed by three other bodies, a line at the end of which descended two smaller ones. At the centre of the motif a distant luminous cluster made up of dots as fine as dust formed a bright mass against the black of the sky. It looked precisely like a commode. Sophia burst out laughing, and almost at once she felt a pang of emotion.

"What do you find so amusing, dear one? Allow me to share your delight," demanded Mathieu, obviously offended.

"Oh, it would take far too long to explain. But do stop worrying about me and marry your Albertine with your soul at peace. Be happy."

"Geraldine."

"I beg your pardon?"

"My fiancée's name is Geraldine."

"Never mind. Marry Geraldine, go forth and multiply. And most of all, don't worry about me."

Without a word Mathieu walked away, his heels clicking along the path. Sophia stayed alone under the black sky, looking for the Pig, the Ear of Corn, and the Hen, and tried to imagine Mr. Pincher's profile.

24 March 1848

Supplies are at their lowest and basically we are reduced to eating Mr. Goldner's tinned meats, of which we open three twenty-pound cans per day and hope for the best. Since we started this diet we have lost some twenty men and the condition of several others has deteriorated. I found myself wondering if it would be better to content ourselves with the meagre ration of sea biscuits we are still able to bake. Who knows, perhaps that often-foul food is part of the cause of our misery. Like the snow we swallow that does nothing but stir up the fire of thirst, sometimes killing. All the same, most of the men, if given the choice of dying with an empty stomach or a full one, will choose to eat what is put before them and not ask any questions. I cannot blame them.

Peddie died four days ago, and I realize that death has become so common that I did not even note the date of MacDonald's, which occurred a fortnight back. I suffer greatly from their absence, as do the rest of the men, who are now deprived of a physician. Adam seems to have taken over, doing the best he can; he assures us that Peddie entrusted to him the contents of his flasks and phials, which he distributes parsimoniously to the sick, who, in any case, do not do any worse. The stock of lemon juice has been exhausted for more than three weeks already but I have the impression that it has been a much longer time since the liquid has not had an effect. I wake up every

morning with the taste of iron in my mouth and I no longer
dare to feel my teeth ever since I dislodged one with a clumsy
movement of my tongue. I know better than anyone the symp-
toms of scurvy, for which there is no remedy among all the
syrups, powders, and decoctions that we brought.

— Aunt?

— Yes.

— May I disturb you for a moment?

— You aren't disturbing me, child. What is it?

— How did you know that you should marry my uncle?

— Why do you ask?

— Because I've never thought about marriage – and I still do not, not exactly, but . . .

— And who has stirred these thoughts? Could it be young de Longchamp? Is he not to marry Albertine Cornell?

— Geraldine.

— As you wish. Is it he who suddenly has you wondering about marriage?

— I read somewhere that if you place a mirror under your pillow, on the morning of the fourteenth day you will see the face of the man you will marry.

— You did? And what face did you see?

— I could not leave the mirror there for fourteen nights, I couldn't sleep with that hard object under my head.

— As for me, I have never, as you know, given any credence to such old wives' tales. I believe that one sees the face of the man one will marry on the morning of one's wedding, when one walks up the aisle on one's father's arm.

— But how do you know that he is the one?

— The other man is the pastor, child.

— Aunt, I'm serious.

— So am I, Sophia. Now listen: you have no need to marry.

Your uncle and I, God be thanked, will leave you a sufficient fortune that you will never have financial difficulties. You will be well able to run a household, travel, even to work should you wish without the hindrance of a husband. So tell me why you would like to enslave your destiny to that of a man?

— Because more and more it seems to me that it already is.

Stella Maris

FOR MONTHS NOW Lady Jane has been besieging the Admiralty, has stood waiting in ill-lit, drafty corridors, bribing secretaries, aides de camp, butlers, and other lesser sorts, insisting, hounding, pursuing, hunting, and, all shame swallowed, has ended up pleading and beseeching. Nothing has any effect. The Admiralty says not a word. The expedition is not in danger; the expedition *cannot* be in danger. The pride of the British Navy is not about to stay imprisoned in a territory from which any whaler at all can extricate himself with his eyes closed. As for previous failures, if indeed one can speak of failures, they are milestones marking the progress of the conquest of this last section of the globe to escape from the grip of the Crown and it is inconceivable that errors committed in the last centuries or past decades should be repeated: indicating the dangers that lie in wait, they are, on the contrary, similar to buoys warning of the presence of shoals, guarantors of the success of the undertaking. It is ridiculous then to dispatch a rescue expedition. One does not set out to rescue heroes.

Lady Jane goes home exhausted, ankles sore from standing

for too long on legs where varicose veins are appearing that were not there the year before, mouth dry from arguing in vain, heart filled not with despondency but with a will, animated first by anger, which grows from day to day and is gradually being steeped in a muted hatred. They will not get rid of her like that. With her swollen feet immersed in a basin of hot water in which Alice has dissolved some Epsom salts, she settles in at her writing desk to write to those who have refused to see her during the day, then to their colleagues, their opposite numbers, their superiors. When these actions prove fruitless, she takes up her pen to beg for help from some American friends, then from vague acquaintances, before appealing to the highest officers and the heads of state of friendly countries who she hopes will in turn exert pressure on the Crown and the British Admiralty, and succeed by bringing shame on the latter where she herself failed by appealing to their honour.

And then one morning in April, while she is sitting at the breakfast table with Sophia, who is rereading to her the list of her appointments for the morning, she receives the news that she has been expecting for months: Edgar Simonton, the American she had met at an inn in the south of France years before, agrees to finance a search and rescue expedition that will leave in a few weeks.

Lady Jane lets the letter drop onto her toast. She leans back in her chair. She would like to tell Sophia that's it, at last they are successful, but she knows that if she opens her mouth she will not be able to produce the slightest sound. She feels tears come to her eyes and stop somewhere between her throat and her nose.

At once, Simonton takes matters in hand, personally making contact with ship-owners, pilots, and stockists, while an army of assistants and young secretaries sees to obtaining the necessary authorizations (of which there are very few) for setting up the operation. Lady Jane puts them in touch with those who over the months have shown themselves willing to come to her assistance, but she can only follow from a distance the preparations, most of which are taking place on another continent. Feverish, she makes lists of urgent matters, of absolutely essential equipment, she dispatches copies of the maps she herself has drawn over the past three years, the last of which, she is certain, shows the route that her husband followed. Panicking, she realizes that the whole story is getting away from her, has already gotten away, that the fate of Sir John rests inexplicably in hands other than hers. Less than one month later, everything is ready, the *Jupiter* is set to weigh anchor in the port of Greenhithe, whence they will cast off in the presence of families and friends of the missing, whom she has personally invited to the event.

AS THE DAYS GO BY, Crozier sees an incredible array of bric-à-brac accumulating on the pack ice, as might be seen in the warehouse of a general store turned upside down by particularly incompetent burglars. Piled up there, baroque, astounding, is an odd collection of objects whose mere presence in this universe of ice defies understanding. Reviewing the absurd mounds, he has to muffle a nervous fit of coughing, but he cannot reconcile himself to order these distraught and bloodless men, whose fever-bright eyes haunt him, to leave behind the final links attaching them to the world that has been theirs and to the existence they are trying with all their might to still believe in. These household trinkets are just so many charms, it is all of England that they will pull behind them, the weight of their country, even if it should lead them directly to their death. Among these growing piles proclaiming with eloquence the superiority of civilization over savage nature are found:

- silver flatware
- undergarments
- small cakes of scented soap
- polish for buttons
- toothbrushes
- 4 Bibles
- bedroom slippers

- sponges

- a copy of *The Vicar of Wakefield*

- empty cigar boxes

- wax seals

- curtain rods

The last-named are, however, simply too preposterous. Taking aside Fitzjames, who, like him, observes these mountains of objects growing hour by hour:

"I am well aware that these wretched dinghies are nearly as heavy empty as full and that we would be well advised to bring along everything that we might need, but seriously, James, I believe we must give up the notion of hanging any sort of curtain during the next few weeks or even the coming months."

Fitzjames attempts a thin smile, something he has not done for weeks.

"No, Francis," he explains, "of all this hodgepodge, the curtain rods may be the only useful things. It was Adam who suggested that we bring them to use as lightning rods when we are alone on an ice floe that stretches out as far as the eye can see, with no shelter, in the middle of a thunderstorm."

Crozier wonders at once why he did not think of it himself. Accordingly, he takes a second look at the rest of the objects there; perhaps each one serves some mysterious purpose that escapes him just now but will be revealed at the opportune moment.

I ASKED ALL THE MEN who had written journals, letters, and memoirs to bring them to me so that we would leave them clearly visible in Sir John's cabin, which strikes me as the place where rescuers would be most likely to look for them. Some refused vehemently, choosing to entrust their writing to the flames in the stove. What they could have noted that was terrible enough that they would rather destroy every sign of their passage, I do not know. I let them do as they wished. What does it matter?

There was, however, something infinitely sad about seeing them line up in front of the cast-iron ogre, hugging in their thin arms a bundle of sheets of paper, notebooks, a journal covered in leather which produced a brief, bright flash before going up in smoke. Though intentional, this *auto-da-fé* is no less abhorrent.

To those who have entrusted their writings to me I promised that I would not read them and I respected that oath. I merely placed on Sir John's desk and bunk, unused since his death, the various notebooks and bundles of papers, some of them accompanied by a note: "For Elizabeth Wilson, 12 Parson Lane, Peterborough," or "Blessed be he who will read these lines."

Feverish, DesVoeux suggested as well that we leave a message in the cairn erected more than a year ago. I did not wish to oppose him, even though I did not and do not see the utility of it. He thought it wise to take the sheet of paper left there some eighteen months before and trace on it, with a trembling hand, a new message that was rolled like a garland around the earlier one. Why in God's name did he not instead use the still blank back of the paper? Did he fear that whoever found it would forget to check the other side? Seeing him turn the sheet over and over abruptly, a quarter-turn each time, to continue his message, I had the impression that he must have been suffering from fever for several days, a feeling that became a certainty when I read the few lines he had written, which one might have thought the work of a man who was drunk. In it mention is made, in an untidy, incomprehensible jumble, of a cairn erected elsewhere by John Ross, of a sheet of paper that had been lost, then found, of a tower that had disappeared. But that, too, is of no importance. There are sufficient documents inside the *Erebus* that attest to our presence and give details of the journey we are undertaking, so I do not stop him from setting off again to entrust those few frenzied words to the stones.

As for me, I cannot bring myself to abandon either to the cold of the deserted ships or to the fire this notebook that has been my confidant ever since we set off, that sometimes seems to me to be the only way to explain why I have not yet lost my mind. I shall take it with me, under my shirt, along with the daguerreotype of Sophia.

H. M. S.hips *Erebus and Terror*
{ Wintered in the Ice in
28 of May 1847 } Lat. 70° 5' N. Long. 98° 23' W

Having wintered in 1846—7 at Beechey Island
in Lat 74° 43' 28" N. Long 91° 39' 15" W After having
ascended Wellington Channel to Lat 77° and returned
by the West side of Cornwallis Island.

Commander

Sir John Franklin commanding the Expedition
All well

Party consisting of 2 Officers and 6 Men
left the Ships on Monday 24th May 47

Gm Gore Lieut
Chas F Des Vaeux Mate

THEY HAVE BEEN WALKING on the pack ice for three weeks, dragging boats that weigh as much as a world, and the readings taken by an incredulous Crozier sometimes reveal at the end of a day spent making painful progress, stooped from effort in this lunar landscape, that not only have they not come the distance anticipated but they have regressed, as the ice moves with an unfavourable current. No doubt their instruments are not absolutely reliable, distorted by their proximity to the magnetic pole, even by the quantity of scrap iron they are pulling behind them like the unwieldy shadow of the country they have forsaken and now refuse obstinately to abandon. It is impossible then to know precisely where they are, and it changes nothing because they know well they are no longer totally on this Earth.

It sometimes takes hours to cross a few yards of ice that seems to be folded onto itself and rumpled like a monstrous piece of fabric to form tremendous solid waves with sharp ridges onto which they must tip the boats in order to go on. Elsewhere, the ice has been transformed into a kind of thick pulp that impedes their steps, and they sink into it up to their knees.

After intense discussions, twenty-two men turned around in the second week of their march and set out again, back towards the ships, taking with them a sloop holding part of the provisions, with DesVoeux leading them. God have mercy on them. Those who have stayed wonder at times what has happened to the others – if they have been able to get back to the *Terror* and the *Erebus*, if they too are racked with hunger, if they have been found by an expedition sent out to search for them, if they are still of this world.

The procession thins out from day to day. All have trouble walking, their muscles feel like open wounds, they are half-blinded by the sun whose dazzling brightness is reflected off the snow that still surrounds them completely. They are weak, starving, but they are not hopeless because in the face of all opposition they continue to advance, even when their walking takes them farther from the goal that they sense in a confused way they will never reach.

The fallen are no longer buried; there is no time or energy for digging the frozen ground to offer them a grave. They are merely covered with snow and at their heads the men make a small pile of stones gathered up nearby, like a tumulus to indicate the presence of prehistoric bones. After a mere three or four hours their skin takes on a bluish tinge reminiscent of the hide of a sea mammal.

Crozier says a few words, always the same ones, to commit their souls to God and beg for mercy for the living, and he places beneath a stone a sheet of paper inscribed with the name, age, and rank of the deceased, as well as the itinerary he himself is preparing to follow with the survivors. He hopes in spite of everything that these improvised cairns will be able to guide rescuers to them before it is too late, but deep in his soul he knows that the path drawn by his men's remains cannot be a path of life. The last time they left behind one of their men, spread out stiffly on the cold ground, Crozier turned around and saw the note he had written with trembling hand fly away, white against the sky.

— THOMAS?

— . . .

— Thomas, are you asleep?

— . . .

— Thomas?

— Yes.

— Were you asleep?

— No.

— Are you cold?

— No.

— Can you move your legs, Thomas? Wiggle your toes.

— . . .

— Come on, try, just wiggle them once.

— . . .

— That's all right. Rest. We'll try again later, once you've warmed up a little. Are you thirsty?

— No.

— I saw her, Thomas, this time I really did see her . . .

— . . .

— You know, the lady in white . . . The one they promised us every day on deck would visit. She's even more beautiful than I'd have thought, with skin as fine as glass and a very sweet voice. She talked to me, Thomas, she told me that soon I would join her and that she was expecting me. Close your eyes, Thomas, and you'll see her too, with her long robe as white as snow . . .

— . . .

— She's waiting for us, Thomas, she's waiting for you . . .
Can you see her?

— . . .

— Go to sleep now.

IT IS GREY on this 8th day of May 1848 when the *Jupiter* is getting ready to cast off. Crowded onto the wharves is a sparse and shivering crowd. The women's faces are drawn, the children stamp their feet and ask to go home. On the water, as on land, a cold wind is blowing and a few drops of rain are falling from a sky swollen with clouds. The crew is assembled on the deck from where it gives a solemn salute. Lady Jane spies Mr. T., in the background and leaning on the ship's rail, a blissful smile on his round face, already savouring the sea air. Then the ship sets off, Simonton shouts something that cannot be heard, the men waving goodbye shrink until they are nothing but minute shapes on a boat no bigger than a thimble. On the wharf only Sophia and Lady Jane, Mr. Bingley and Mr. Darcy are left.

11 May 1848

THE NIGHTS ARE MORE difficult than the days. The men dig rough-and-ready shelters in the snow or cluster inside the sloops, where morning finds them curled up and huddled together, shivering, in the midst of the incredible jumble.

The Polar star shines all through the night, a useless guide. The Star of the Sea resembles a small eye, always open, impassive, above our heads. It is most often at night that people die, alone amid their fellow creatures lost in their nightmares. At times it is impossible to unfold the frozen bodies and they are committed to the earth like that, knees against chin.

In the morning, muscles are stiff, joints painful, the slightest effort is torture. Yesterday, four seamen refused to start walking again. They stayed back, sitting in the snow, dazed, gazing hollow-eyed at the provisions and the few tools that I ordered left for them. One was hanging on desperately to a fork which he held tightly in his right hand; another was swaying back and forth, a smile on his lips, singing softly to himself.

18 May 1848

Tomorrow will mark three years since we left Greenhithe. We will have gone around the Sun three times and at the same time remained cruelly motionless.

We pitched a tent where we will leave those who cannot go on. We spend one last night with them before setting off again, with the impression – accurate, too accurate – of keeping a vigil with a man in agony whom we shall abandon in the morning to the death that is lying in wait for him. We let them have more than half of the provisions, rifles, and tools, but they are so weakened that they will be unable to hunt or fish, should they even have learned how, which is not the case. Most have trouble even taking a few steps. They have asked us to leave Neptune with them, but from the brightness of their eyes at that moment I realized that they wanted neither his company nor his protection but, rather, his meat. I shall not leave them the dog. I shall not leave them the dog but I am abandoning defenceless men to starving men. Tonight I looked one last time at the faces of those whom I shall no doubt never see again, for whom I was responsible and whom I have led to their death in this land of ice. Their noses, foreheads, cheeks are blackened by the cold which has robbed them of toes, fingers, an ear. Their teeth have come loose in their gums streaked with blood. Some have virtually lost their eyesight, victims of snow blindness which afflicts eyes strained from too much whiteness. These beings, now totally stripped of that which made them men, toothless, incapable of feeding themselves or of moving, seem to have returned, through some hideous irony of fate, to the state of nursling; they will leave this world as they entered it, dispossessed of everything.

I dare not imagine what will become of them in the days to come.

All I can hope for is that their death be gentle.

Some cry in hushed tones while we prepare to set off in the deathly pale light of dawn. Others groan or let out moans that have nothing human about them. We walk away without turning around.

21 June 1848

Once again we must leave our companions behind, without even a tent for protection from the elements or rations worthy of the name to keep them alive while they wait for us to come back with help, or for a group of Esquimaux to take them under their wing, or for a search expedition to discover them.

For shelter we leave them the last sloop, which is too heavy to be dragged by three men, and the bulk of what it contains: tea, chocolate, useless cufflinks, and a Bible that has miraculously survived various prunings. Wilks stuffs a bit of paper into my hand which I think at first is a letter bidding final farewell to his fiancée. Unfolding it I discover some lines written with a trembling hand:

> *Das reyd... who Eboud yna sah ohw rof eva trofmoC ta evarg eht, guilts yht si erehw htaeD O*

There must be some meaning to that but I do not have time to elucidate the message and I content myself with carefully folding the paper and slipping it into my pocket as if it were an amulet. Fitzjames and Adams lavish pointlessly some final attention on those we are abandoning to the cold.

It occurs to me only today, while we pursue this march of which no one knows whether it will lead us straight to death or to safety, that in recent days we have crossed the Passage we set out in search of more than a thousand days ago. It does not appear on any map, is not drawn on any chart; nothing testifies to its existence apart from, in the distance, the bodies of those who have fallen and have not got up.

Hornby and Thomas are conscious when we leave and they watch us disappear, eyes wide open.

There are now only three of us under the white of the sky.

THAT MORNING LADY JANE rose early, dispatched quickly and without much pleasure her breakfast, which she took alone, Sophia not having fallen asleep until dawn. She had dressed immediately and given the domestics their instructions for the day. As early as ten o'clock, then, when a weak spring sun was coming in the window, spreading a pale light, she was at her desk, pen in hand. Only now, for the first time since Sir John's departure, the words did not come, the ideas did not jostle in her mind from where they usually gushed as from an inexhaustible spring.

She sat for a long moment disconcerted, then forced herself to inscribe a few platitudes on the paper; she crumpled it almost immediately into a ball which she tossed to the floor, where it landed on Mr. Darcy's muzzle. The dog let out a little yelp and walked away decorously.

Lady Jane's irritation was threatening to give way to anger. She took a deep breath, looked around the sitting room where her treasures were displayed, considered with an expression half severe, half satisfied the bundles of letters, cards, maps, drawings, and sketches that she had produced over these past years and of which she had made copies that she had confided to Mr. Simonton, being very careful to keep the originals in her possession.

Feeling dizzy, as though she were standing on the edge of a cliff, she tried to shake herself. In an impatient motion she spilled the cup of tea she had set on the desk and stared as if hypnotized at the amber liquid spreading across her maps, blurring the delicate lines of watercolours she had drawn there over the years. Rivers that ran to the sea, mountains, straits, lakes and streams, coasts, islands and peninsulas, real or imaginary, melted into a single liquid stain that drowned the Arctic territory altogether.

Author's Note

The preceding narrative does not claim to be anything but a novel. Although partly inspired by genuine events, and although some characters are based on real persons, it claims neither objectivity nor historical accuracy and belongs completely to the realm of fiction.

I have, however, consulted both contemporary books about the Franklin expedition and the Northwest Passage and a certain number of old works on electricity, magnetism, and explorations. In several there were passages I couldn't resist the urge to transcribe faithfully, offering them to readers just as they were written at the time.

The very first paragraph, which deals with the possibility of freezing sea water, is taken practically verbatim from *Discovery and Adventures in the Polar Seas and Regions: with illustrations of their climate, geology, and natural history,* published by Sir John Leslie in 1881; it is also the source of John Barrow's instructions to John Franklin.

The reader will have recognized in *Journey to the Moon* my (rather pathetic) dramatic adaptation of *États et Empires de la Lune,* by Hector Savinien de Cyrano de Bergerac. (The translator made grateful use of Andrew Brown's elegant translation, *Journey to the Moon.*)

The introduction and the brief excerpt from *The Veils* were published in 1815 by Eleanor Porden, who would later marry John Franklin.

The lines attributed to James Ross are from his journal, quoted by Pierre Berton in *The Arctic Grail.*

From the second volume of *Leçons sur l'électricité et le magnétisme,* by Élie Nicolas Mascart and J. Joubert (1882), I took the illustrations of instruments used for magnetic readings, along with explanations and formulæ related to that process.

The document in six languages in which the members of the expedition twice refer to their progress was found in 1859 at Victory Point on King William Island (at the time known as King William's Land, since it was discovered only later that it was surrounded by water). It is one of the only written documents that testifies to the fate of the members of the expedition still alive on April 25, 1848. Another note was found next to a skeleton wearing a steward's uniform, not far from the mouth of the Peffer River; written backwards, it consisted of a few lines reproduced on page 260. The words "O Death, where is thy sting," are from Corinthians 15:55. All quotations from the Bible are from the King James Version.

I relied as well on various other sources, linguistic as well as gastronomic.

The definition of the word "tea" that Crozier finds in an etymological dictionary is very close to that in the *Robert historique de la langue française* dictionary.

For adventurous cooks who have twenty-one days to dedicate to the execution of a dessert and who wish to embark on making a plum pudding, a recipe, inspired by the one found at www.theworldwidegourmet.com, is provided on page 268–269. Bon appétit!

Acknowledgements

This novel would never have seen the light of day without the encouragement and support of a number of people. I am grateful to my first readers, Nadine Bismuth, François Ricard, and Yvon Rivard; their comments helped improve it considerably. Thanks to Jean Bernier for his irrepressible love of Bach. And to Antoine Tanguay of Les Éditions Alto whose confidence and enthusiasm are contagious and who turned a manuscript into a book.

Thanks to Lara Hinchberger and the entire team at McClelland and Stewart for believing that this novel could also exist in English, and to Sheila Fischman who agreed to lend her talent to the task.

Thanks to Fred, for everything, forever.

Plum Pudding

INGREDIENTS

9 oz currants
9 oz sultanas
2 teaspoons candied lemon peel
2 teaspoons candied grapefruit peel
4 teaspoons candied orange peel
9 oz candied cherries
9 oz candied cranberries
4 cups rum
4 oz blanched almonds
18 oz finely chopped suet
8 oz rye bread crumbs
4 oz brown sugar
½ teaspoon powdered cinnamon
½ teaspoon grated nutmeg
½ teaspoon powdered ginger
½ teaspoon ground cloves
a pinch of salt
4 tablespoons brandy
1 cup milk
2 tablespoons butter
4 oz flour
2 teaspoons baking powder
6 large eggs, lightly beaten
juice of one orange
juice of one lemon

Brandy Butter
9 oz unsalted butter
2 oz brandy
zest of 1 orange

Chop finely raisins, and candied peel and fruit. Pour onto mixture four cups of rum and set aside for 48 hours. Drain and reserve rum.

Combine all ingredients but eggs. Add ¼ cup reserved rum and the juice of one orange and one lemon. Cover bowl with cheesecloth soaked in rum and set aside for 21 days. Stir mixture once a day, adding a little rum if necessary to keep the mixture loose.

If the dough becomes too firm, lighten it with a glass of ale; if too liquid, add a little flour and stir gently.

In a pudding mould, place a large piece of cheesecloth with both sides buttered and floured. Add eggs to the batter. Pour the mixture into the mould and fold the four corners of the cheesecloth over the dough. Take a piece of parchment and cover.

Place pudding in oven, in a large pan half-filled with water. Bake for 6 hours at a very low temperature, checking the water level now and then.

Remove pudding from mould and allow to cool.

Cover with clean tea towel and a sheet of parchment and leave in a cool place to ripen for at least one month. (The pudding will only improve if left to age longer.)

On Christmas Day, bake pudding for 3 or 4 hours. Turn out.

Set aflame with brandy or cognac and serve with brandy butter.

© Martine Doyon

DOMINIQUE FORTIER was born in 1972. She holds a Ph.D. in literature from McGill University, and is a respected editor and literary translator. *On the Proper Use of Stars*, her debut novel, was first published in Quebec in 2008 as *Du bon usage des étoiles* and was shortlisted for the French language Governor General's Award for Fiction, the Prix des libraries du Québec, the Grand prix littéraire Archambault, and the Prix Senghor. It is being adapted for the screen by Jean-Marc Vallée (*C.R.A.Z.Y., The Young Victoria*). Dominique's second novel, *Les larmes de saint Laurent*, was published to great acclaim in Quebec in May 2010. She lives in Montreal.

SHEILA FISCHMAN's translation of *On the Proper Use of Stars* was shortlisted for the Governor General's Literary Award for French to English Translation, and is nominated for the American Literary Translators Association National Translation Award. Sheila is the award-winning literary translator of well over a hundred works, by such authors as Hubert Aquin, Anne Hébert, Jacques Poulin, and Gaétan Soucy. Sheila is a Chevalier de l'Ordre national du Québec and a member of the Order of Canada. She lives in Montreal.